BLUE LORRIES

BLUE LORRIES

By Radwa Ashour

Translated by Barbara Romaine

دار بلومزبري - مؤسسة قطر للنشر
BLOOMSBURY
QATAR FOUNDATION
PUBLISHING

مؤسسة قطر
Qatar Foundation

First published in English in 2014 by
Bloomsbury Qatar Foundation Publishing
Qatar Foundation
PO Box 5825
Doha
Qatar
www.bqfp.com.qa

First published in Arabic in 2008 as *Farag* by Dar el Shorouk

ISBN 9789992194485

Typeset by Hewer Text UK Ltd, Edinburgh
Printed and bound in Great Britain by CPI Group (UK) Ltd,
Croydon CR0 4YY

Chapter one

The little girl catches a fever

C AIRO STATION. I LENGTHEN my stride, all but running to catch up with my mother. I'm afraid to let her get even one step ahead of me. 'Why are you holding on to my hand so tightly?' she hisses. 'It hurts!' She tries to extricate her hand from my grasp, but I hold on even tighter.

My mother is busy talking to the fat woman holding a baby, who is making the trip with us. There on the railway platform, where we wait for our train to pull in, an enormous man with thick moustaches and white hair smiles at me and asks my name. I turn my face away. When our eyes meet again he smiles and says, 'You're a very pretty girl!'

'Say "thank you" to Monsieur,' my mother tells me in French. I pretend to busy myself with tightening my shoe-laces, and my mother goes back to her conversation with the fat woman. I turn to the man and stick my tongue out at him.

It wasn't just the crowds, or the noise, or the hubbub, but the persistent, ruthless destruction of everything I had built up in my imagination during the past few days. The trip had obsessed me. I thought about it, talked about it, prepared for it, and, in my imagination, assembled the details of it. I hovered over the great basket in which my mother was packing food, pointing out items she had left out, adjusting, suggesting, adding things. In secret I got my own special things ready – the ones I would share with him – stashing them in my small satchel: my portrait in my school uniform; the notebook, three of whose pages were adorned with gold stars; two chocolate bars.

'Mama, will he recognise me?'

'Of course!'

'But I've got a lot bigger, haven't I?'

'Of course!'

'How much?'

'What?'

'How much bigger am I?'

'Six inches, maybe more.'

'Was my hair long or short when he left?'

'It was short.'

'Do you think he'll like me better in plaits? Should I cut my hair or leave it long? Or maybe he'd like a ponytail better! I'll wear my red dress – it's so pretty!'

'We'll take that one with us for you to wear the next day.'

It took my mother half a day to persuade me to wear a different dress for the journey. What she said sounded reasonable enough, and I didn't disagree; it was just that it meant starting the journey in a way that was different from what I had imagined, different from what I wanted, and I began to feel extremely cross. I hated the other dress, hated the touch of it against my skin – it felt prickly to me, as if made out of thorns. For a moment, at the railway station, I thought about taking it off.

My imagination told me – and so did my mother – that the way to him was strewn with roses: an express train, speeding past fields of green. My mother got out an enormous red book and opened it to the map of Egypt. Pointing to a place near the tip of the inverted pyramid, she said, 'We'll take the train from here –' and with her finger she traced along the line representing the Nile, '– to here. And we'll get off at Asyut, in Upper Egypt.'

'Upper Egypt?' I burst out laughing. 'But you moved your finger *down*!'

She started to explain, but I cut her off. 'Where are the trees? I don't see any trees or animals!'

'They don't appear on the map, but you'll see them for yourself: date palms, sycamores, willows, eucalyptus, and fields of cotton and maize and clover – and you'll see cows and water buffalo, too, and sheep and goats, camels and donkeys, and cattle egrets . . . you'll see them all from the train window, settled there beside me in your seat as if you were at a film. And just like at the cinema, someone will come by with cold drinks for sale, and I'll buy you something.'

She went back to the map. She moved her finger to the left, far from the line showing the Nile. 'The car will bring us to Papa across the desert. You'll see the desert – the desert is amazing!'

'Can I colour the map?'

'In the book?'

My mother must have been in an exceptionally good mood, because after her question, which sounded like a refusal, there was silence for a moment, and then she stated the rule emphatically: 'The atlas isn't a children's book – we don't draw or colour in it.' But then she laughed, 'Well, all right,' and stipulated, 'just this once!'

3

My mother had opened the door, and now my imagination ran wild, between fields of green and deserts of yellow, and a friendly zoo that needed no fences or cages. I saw a sweet-faced donkey approach my window and look at me, I reached out and patted its head and we talked to each other. Maybe some of the animals would decide to come with me and meet my father. In my imagination, the train would speed along and the sweet-faced donkey would be sitting beside me, along with a black she-goat that had become my friend, and with a cattle egret settled on my shoulder.

'Mama, can we bring food for the animals?'

'What animals?'

'The animals we'll meet along the way?'

'The train won't stop!'

'Can't it stop for a little while, so we can spend time with the animals?'

'But we'd be late to meet Papa!'

'Can we stop to pick him a bouquet of flowers from the fields?'

'The driver won't permit that.'

'Yes he will, I'll ask him very nicely and I'll smile. He'll think I'm a nice girl, wearing a pretty red dress, and he'll say, "Certainly!"'

'That's impossible.'

'It's not impossible, it could happen – really!'

Then, on arrival at our destination, I would hand a bouquet of beautiful flowers to my father and see the laughter in his eyes as he spread his arms wide-open to hug me. I would introduce him to my friends, the animals.

The path of our return journey would be likewise strewn with roses. The Director would say, 'Go with your daughter and your wife – they are very nice.'

4

I broke into song: '*Salma ya salaama, ruhna wa geena bis-salaama.*'

'You're off-key, Nada!' my mother shouted from the next room. She picked up where I left off, and hummed the melody for me. 'Like this,' she said, repeating it again.

'You're ruining my singing,' I told her. 'Who said I wanted a music lesson? Besides, you don't know the song, and you pronounce the words wrong.' I mimicked her French accent, '*Ghuhna wa geena bis-salaama!*'

I said the last few words only in an undertone, making a dash for the toilet, where I locked myself in and sang at the top of my lungs, while the twofold pleasures of speaking my mind and outwitting my mother converged.

The train didn't bode well. There was the wooden seat, whose roughness I could feel when I sat on it; the window-shade that didn't work – we couldn't open it; and the odour of human sweat, commingled with indistinguishable smells of various foods. And the shrieking baby – it screamed until its mother silenced it with her breast. As soon as she did that and the baby quieted, she resumed her conversation with my mother in a voice so loud I couldn't stand it. I whispered in my mother's ear, 'Can't you ask her to lower her voice a little – it's annoying!' My mother tossed me a glance that told me I was the one who had better be quiet.

The train, with its relentless clamour, its window stuck shut, seemed stifling. I tried to sleep, but I couldn't, so I distracted myself by imagining the little mice in the room that the neighbours' daughter had told me about – she said it was a scary, dark room in which children were locked up as punishment. She said she was afraid of mice – why should she be afraid of them? Such gentle little creatures. Silently I talked to the mice, and listened to their replies. But the baby interrupted our conversation with a new round of wailing.

I shouted at my mother in French, 'Shut that stupid baby up, or I'll throw it out the window!'

She said in an unmistakably threatening tone, 'Mind your manners, or we'll go back home and forget about visiting Papa!' Then she added in a whisper, 'The lady knows a bit of French – what if she understood what you said?'

'I want to go to the toilet.'

My mother took me to the toilet. She told me to avoid sitting on the seat of the commode.

'How?'

'Just don't touch it! It's not clean. Leave some space, even if it's only a little bit, between your bottom and the seat.'

'I can't!'

'Like this.' My mother put her arms round my waist, so that my weight was supported by my legs and her arms. I emptied my bladder.

I laughed and said, 'That wasn't so bad!' Then, as I followed her back to our seats, I said, 'It's not that hard. I can do it by myself next time.'

But the next time I said I was 'going to the toilet', it wasn't to relieve myself; I had decided that I wasn't going to put up any longer with the dress I'd been made to wear. I went into the toilet, took off the dress, folded it up, and went back out in my underwear. Let my mother say what she liked, let her shout as much as she pleased, she was barmy anyway, yelling all the time for no reason – now she'd have a reason. When I got back to my seat, my mother was engrossed in talking to the fat woman. I sat down calmly and closed my eyes, willing myself to sleep. And in fact I dozed off.

As soon as we entered the hotel room the fat woman sighed deeply and pulled down the covers in order to lay the baby down. 'Bedbugs!' she exclaimed. And with that she took out a container of insecticide, gave the baby to my mother, and instructed us to leave the room. A few minutes later she joined us, reclaimed her son, and we went down to the hotel restaurant.

'Mama, the restaurant smells bad!'

'Mama, the tablecloth's dirty!'

'Mama, the food's nasty!'

My mother shouted at me in front of the fat woman and her baby, so I turned my face away from her and announced that I wasn't hungry. I pressed my lips tightly together, crossed my arms on my chest, and stared fixedly at the opposite wall until they finished eating. Then we moved into the sitting room next to the restaurant, but I kept silent and wouldn't look in their direction, until we went upstairs to the room. We opened the windows, but the smell of insecticide was overwhelming. I told my mother I was going to suffocate, but she said I would just have to bear it. I didn't see why. Then she gave me a bath and dressed me in my nightgown. She pulled down the covers. The sheet had a big dark stain on it, and I refused to lie down on it. My mother laid a clean, white towel over the stain and said, '*Voilà!* Now you can lie down!'

I refused. I stayed where I was, sitting on the chair. Everyone else went to sleep, and in the silent room I was able once more to recall the little mice and continue my conversation with them. Talking to mice was so much nicer than talking to Mama. I sat cross-legged on the chair, and we carried on talking until I drifted off to sleep.

We left the hotel that had so thoroughly disgusted me, with its corridors and vestibule dimly lit by a yellowish glow. Despite the desolation and the enveloping gloom as we hired a taxi, I was complaisant. For my mother had at last permitted me to put on the red dress. She had released my hair from its plait, replacing it with a ponytail, which she secured with an elastic band and tied with a ribbon of white satin. When my mother decided to sit next to the car door and put me between herself and the fat woman, I didn't protest.

The darkness was impenetrable, utterly lightless except for the tiny stars in the sky. I stared at them continuously through the window, until the darkness faded to purple, then lilac, then yellow. After that we passed into pure orange, as an intense sun lit up the sand dunes that extended away from us on either side, interrupted here and there by barren hills of dark-grey or reddish rock. (My mother is right, no doubt, that I have taken this road many times, for its features are sharply defined: why then can I call to mind the memory of only a single journey?)

All at once I exclaimed, 'Mama, I'm happy!' I turned to the fat woman, smiled at her, and asked her what her son's name was. I set about playing with him, making him laugh, and then I asked whether I could hold him. His mother positioned him in my arms, gently drawing my right arm around his little body, and guiding my left hand to support his head. I was thrilled by my own ability to hold a baby correctly, and I fell to prattling to him, calling him by name, petting and jiggling him. I loved this connection with him, and felt he was even nicer than the mice I'd amused myself with the

8

night before. Then all at once he was sick on me. His mother laughed, and I burst into tears. I cried until we arrived, telling my mother, 'I'm going to my father in a dirty dress, and this horrid lady laughed! What's so funny about a nasty little boy who is sick on beautiful dresses?' I turned to the woman and said, 'He was sick on me!'

'Child,' she replied, 'he wasn't sick, he just spat up. All babies do that! And the dress is lovely on you!' She laughed, and I cried even harder.

My mother later said it was the longest I'd ever cried in my life, that I cried from six o'clock in the morning until we arrived at eight.

The taxi stopped in front of a great, sprawling single-storey building, with small, barred windows. On top of the building were men armed with rifles. Three guards came out, and one of them asked, 'Visiting?'

'Visiting.'

'Permits?'

He took the folded papers that were handed to him. He disappeared, then came back. 'Come along.'

In a vast room furnished with small tables and a lot of chairs we sat down to wait. Two men in strange clothes appeared. One of them rushed toward me and tried to catch me up. I struggled against him.

What a reunion: I didn't recognise my own father!

I say I didn't recognise my father, because this is what my mother kept repeating throughout the months that followed, and in later years it was the story my father recounted, laughing as if it were a joke. But a twitch in the corner of his left eye told a different tale. How does the mind record what has happened, by what logic is memory subverted, delivering me to a recollection of events that is the opposite of what really happened? During the succeeding months I thought it was my father who hadn't recognised me. Every time I cried (because my mother scolded me or because my teacher disciplined me, or because a toy I loved broke in my hands), the tears would be automatically transformed to sorrow that my father hadn't known his Nada, that he had forgotten me, that he didn't want me. I would repeat these things to myself, my sobs rising in a crescendo.

Chapter two

Which of the two men is better?

I HAVE TO RECONSTRUCT IN my imagination what occurred at our home at dawn on the first of January 1959. I was asleep, and didn't witness any part of the event. I woke in the morning to my mother's pale face. I was surprised at how preoccupied she was with tidying the house – she worked rapidly, nervously, mechanically, as if it were essential that, by some specific time, she do away with the clutter and disorder all over the place. In the days that followed, although no one said a word to me about what had happened, everything around me appeared strange and bewildering: my father's absence, the expression on my mother's face and the jarring rhythm of her speech, the sudden arrival of my grandmother and paternal aunt who came from Upper Egypt to stay with us for several days – which had never happened before – the frequent visitors and their whispered conversations among themselves and with my mother: conversations that broke off abruptly any time I turned up in their vicinity. Then those evasive answers each time I asked about my father: 'He's travelling.' 'He'll be back soon.' 'His job required him to travel unexpectedly, and he didn't want to wake you up.' 'He'll stay there for a while.' 'We'll go and visit him soon.' 'His work is far away, we can't go there now!' Answers that proved there were no answers, fashioning around me a dense fog that only intensified my fear and confusion.

One morning I awoke in tears. 'Why did you lie to me? You didn't tell me my father died like the rabbit!'

'Your father's not dead! He's fine, and he's coming back!'

'You're lying – he died like the rabbit. When I went to sleep the rabbit was on the balcony, and when I woke up the rabbit was gone! And it's the same, just the same with Papa!'

My father had bought the rabbit for me, and my mother had taught me how to feed it and care for it. Then one morning it vanished, and my mother told me it had died.

This day my mother had to sit beside me on the bed and have a long talk with me about an important and learned man who understood many things, and said matters must proceed in this manner and not that, and this was right and that was wrong. And about officers who held a different opinion – thinking the way a headmaster thinks, that the system must be run their way. They disagreed with him, and so they put him in prison.

'What's a prison?'

'It's a place that's locked up so you can't get out.'

'Like the lion at the zoo?'

'Like the lion at the zoo.'

'What happens next?'

'I'm not telling you a story. I'm explaining why Papa doesn't live with us right now. He hasn't died – he'll stay there for a little while, and then they'll let him come home.'

I found it all quite perplexing; yet it was the beginning of awareness, and of a need to compare my own situation with that of others. These comparisons would preoccupy me in the years that followed, often placing me in uncomfortable positions. I wasn't alone in this, for I recall that Mona Anis – whose father, Dr Abdel Azim Anis, was my father's colleague, both of them university professors and both incarcerated in the same prison – confided to me that one of Abdel Nasser's sons was her classmate. I told her I wanted to meet him, so that I could ask him why his father had put our fathers in prison, and if he didn't know we could ask him to find out. Mona never got the chance to introduce me to the boy, for her school was in Manshiyat al-Bakri, while mine was in Garden City. But she did relate to me a detailed account of what passed between her and the classroom teacher. Mona said, 'I asked the teacher in front of the whole class, "Whose father is better, his or mine?"' When the teacher didn't answer, Mona said, 'Papa's a university professor, he has a doctoral degree, and he used to teach at London University. When Britain attacked Egypt, he organised a demonstration in England. He left his job there and said, "I'm going back home to help my country." *His* father's an officer, and it's true he fought in the war for Palestine and staged the revolution, but he doesn't have a doctorate, and he's never taught at London University! *My* father is better educated, and he's more knowledgeable!' Mona insisted that the teacher acknowledge before all the pupils that her father was the better man. The teacher, however, said, 'This won't do. All of you here are my children, and it wouldn't be right for me to say that one person is better than another, or that one person's father is better than another's.'

I asked her in astonishment, and with a good deal of admiration, 'You said that in class, in front of all the boys and girls?' Mona crossed her legs, spoke more loudly and said,

'Yes, I did,' and she repeated the story in all its particulars. Now I admired her even more. She was three years older than I was and several inches taller, and whenever I declared that she was my friend I felt an access of pride, as if this friendship lent some of her height to my childish body, and conferred upon me a part of her authoritative mien. She knew lots of things, which she discussed in detail, while I looked on in wonder, confident that she was my superior in her wisdom and her understanding of the world, and, between us, the more capable of interpreting and unravelling its mysteries.

One day Mona visited us with her mother, and she read me a poem her father had written for her. The poem so unsettled me that I stopped listening to it, distracted by the question: Why didn't my own father send me a poem? Did her father love her more than mine loved me? I couldn't keep the question to myself – I confided it to my mother. She laughed, and said, 'Her father knows how to write poetry; your father doesn't!'

How was I to apply this new piece of information to the comparison between my father and Gamal Abdel Nasser? What reasoning could I bring to bear? I found myself thinking, 'He doesn't know how to write poetry to his daughter – maybe he's no better or smarter than Nasser.' But then the scales would tip the other way, and I would think, 'But my father has a doctorate from the Sorbonne, he was a university professor, so surely he knows and understands more than officers do, and his political goals are superior to theirs.'

My father wasn't there, though, while Nasser's name, his voice, and his picture cropped up everywhere, on a daily, even an hourly, basis. He was celebrated in songs that I loved, whose lyrics I could recall, and I would sing them, whether I got the melody right or not. He wasn't merely a leader, merely a president. He was a topic of conversation in every household and on every street and in every school – quite simply he pervaded the very space in which we grew and took shape, as if he were water or air or earth or sunbeams that we absorbed as a matter of course, becoming what we became. It was Nasser who brought us up, proud though I was of my kinship to my father. When I pronounced my own name, my voice would be normal, or perhaps softer than normal, on 'Nada,' but then it would grow louder as I went on to say, 'Abdel Qadir Selim,' as if 'Nada' were no more than a prop, or a point of entry, or a stepping-stone for the name that should be prominent and unmistakable. I don't think any of these ideas ever occurred to me when I was that age, but I remember clearly what happened when I watched Nasser deliver a speech, following his words and staring intently at his posture and his facial expressions; suddenly I said to my mother, 'Mama, doesn't he look like Papa?'

'No,' my mother replied.

Then, 'Well, maybe he looks like him.'

When I went to bed. I tried to call to mind an image of my father, the better to make a comparison, but my imagination ran up against a blank wall. I tried a second time, and a third. I didn't realise what had happened until I found my mother kneeling by the bed, pale-faced, asking me, 'What's the matter, why are you screaming?'

This incident may have been a repetition of a previous one that occurred some years earlier, maybe a few months after my father's arrest. I remember my mother kneeling by the bed, then carrying me to her big bed. She fetched a red metal box, opened it up and took out pictures of my father to show me. As she picked up each one, she would say, 'Here's Papa on such-and-such a day . . .' Presently I calmed down and chose one of the pictures, a large one in which my father's features were clear, and then I went back to bed. Instead of lying face-down the way I normally did, I lay on my back and held the picture up before my face. I drifted off, still holding the picture, and when I awoke in the morning I found it bent at the edges, perhaps because I had been lying on it. This started me off on another bout of crying and irritability.

Whether or not they resembled each other wasn't the question, even if they were of the same generation, sharing Upper Egyptian origins, and both embodying the idea of 'father'. The first was a generic father, held in common by all, while the second was the individual, actual father – with a hop, skip, and a jump I could be in his bedroom, open up his wardrobe, and run my hands over the neatly folded shirts in one of its drawers.

I was nine years old when a classmate of mine – having suddenly found it necessary to express her nationalist zeal – said, 'Your mother's French. The French attacked Egypt as part of the Tripartite Aggression. From now on we're not friends.' Although she had caught me off-guard, without a moment's thought I heard myself say to her, '*I'm* the one who doesn't want to be friends with *you*. You have bad breath, and it's not as if you were poor and couldn't afford toothpaste – you go to an expensive French school. And by the way, our *bawaab*'s wife, who comes sometimes to clean our house, doesn't use toothpaste, but she rinses her mouth regularly and her breath smells lovely. Her clothes are clean as well. You're horrid – I don't want to talk to you.'

Quick though I was with an answer, her words took me aback. (The comment 'it's not as if you were poor', and the allusion to a preference for the wife of our *bawaab*, were like a goal scored in her net, proving that I had learned the lesson my mother taught me. She was careful of my upbringing in matters like these, admonishing me, 'A certain little girl – the *bawaab*'s daughter, let's say – is the same age as you, and by chance – purely by chance – you're privileged to wear the dress you wear, while it's not given to her to wear one like it. It may be that she's better than you. We'll have to wait and see what you do with what you have, and what she may do in spite of the hardship she faces. And that boy' – she was referring to a child my age, clothed in rags, who stood at the traffic light selling packets of tissues – 'is an innocent victim. You get more, he gets less.' She had an endless supply of these sermons, adducing as evidence my clothes, food, and – the thing she harped on most insistently and distressingly – chocolate. I would grow fidgety with all her instruction, or I might become anxious in the expectation that she would forbid me to buy chocolate. My mother was like a machine, incessantly, tirelessly producing her educational directives, and at that age I could not know anything of the ideological basis for such directives.)

But what the girl had said unsettled me. At lunch I asked, 'Mama, why did France attack Egypt in 1956?'

'Because France is an imperialist state, and it had begun to lose the countries it occupied, so it became more aggressive. It had been defeated in Indochina and . . .'

'What's Indochina?'

'A country called Vietnam, in Asia – I'll show it to you on the map.'

She was about to get up to go fetch the book, but I persuaded her to put off fussing with the atlas (another of the pedagogical tools to which she frequently had recourse).

'No, carry on.'

'Well, France was confronting a revolution in Algeria, and Nasser was supporting this revolution, and moreover he had nationalised the canal. He was a threat to France's interests, and they wanted to get rid of him.'

'Were you on the side of the French when they attacked Egypt?'

She laughed. 'How could I have been on their side?'

'But you're French!'

'Are you in favour of your father's detention?'

'Of course not.'

'So you don't agree with everything your country's government does!'

I understood, and I laughed. Then I told her about the horrid girl. She said, 'There's no need to cut her off. You could have explained things to her.'

'I want nothing to do with her,' I announced firmly. 'She has bad breath, and besides, I don't care to keep company with fools – if people saw me with her they might think I'm as stupid as she is. That would be bad for my reputation!'

I particularly emphasised the part about my reputation, and my mother laughed, just as I had intended her to do. And when she laughed, so did I.

My mother did get up to fetch the atlas, and began to instruct me purposefully on the map of Asia and the location of Indochina, reinforcing geography with history. She told me in which years France entered and departed from Indochina, and how . . . and now it was America's turn . . .

and all the while I nodded my head, saying, 'Yes, it's very clear,' although in fact nothing was clear, for the simple reason that my head was full of a new question: My mother had said, 'Nasser constituted a threat to the French, and therefore they attacked him.' This bit of information assumed a powerful significance in the debate that preoccupied me, as to which man was right – the president who had arrested and detained my father, or my father, whose opinions had led to his incarceration and his being exiled from his family for all these years.

Chapter three

Translation problems I

JOKING WITH MY FRIENDS, I said, 'I was a translation "gofer" – I learned the craft by the time I could walk!'

I left it at that, for to go into detail would have required that I tell them the story of my life. They knew my mother was French, and that I was born and raised in a bilingual household, but none of them knew that, from as far back as I can remember, I assumed the role of interpreter. 'What are they saying?' my mother would ask suddenly. 'What does the man mean?' 'What is the lady trying to say?' So I would translate. 'What's so funny about that?' she might demand. And I would explain.

Or someone would ask me, 'What's your mother saying? What does she want?' And I would translate. My paternal aunt might come to visit us, and I would be the linguistic intermediary between her and my mother. But I faced the most difficult trials in the many encounters between my mother and my paternal grandmother. My grandmother never left her village until she was past the age of seventy, and she spoke in a rural idiom that was difficult to understand – in retrospect I think it was eloquent – studded with proverbs, parables, and quotations from the Qur'an. In my childhood, translating what she said was a real challenge, like decoding a cipher. I had to think about it first, then pass along the easier bits, pouncing on the parts I could manage and summarising the rest in order to fill in the blanks. I settled for the gist, or I improvised something that would fit well enough into the general context. But sometimes she defied such devices. My grandmother might produce one little phrase that I could not understand, even though the words themselves were clear enough. For example, 'When we visited you after they took away your father, a twelvemonth ago, in *Toba* . . .' and I would stop short, perplexed, my mind casting about in a vain attempt to solve the riddle. I knew that 'a twelvemonth ago', in my grandmother's parlance, simply meant 'last year', but what on earth was '*toba*', and what could 'in *toba*' signify? Was it the name of a place where they'd taken my father? Did they make him sit on some kind of brick? But she had said 'in' and not 'on'! I decided it was too much trouble to ask the meaning of '*toba*', since even a witless three-year-old knew that '*toba*' meant 'brick'; nor did I see fit to translate the sentence verbatim for my mother, lest she tell me I was stupid or that my grandmother had gone senile. At the time I knew nothing of the rural custom of using the Coptic names for the months. So I kept quiet. Then, when my mother wanted to know why I didn't translate my grandmother's words, imagination came to my rescue. 'She said that your frock is very pretty. Also, she noticed that your new eyeglasses suit you better than the old ones.'

After the episode of the mourning period, I learned that aphorism about the sieve – which is to say, I learned to strain out those contaminants that would certainly have fouled the waters flowing between the two sides, while at the same time

I took care that neither of them should suspect my interference. So if my mother was glowering, I would hold back something my grandmother had said and abridge the rest. If my aunt went on the offensive and severely criticised my mother, the attack would be converted in the translated version into a mild rebuke. If my mother was the aggressor, I would whitewash her comments before passing them along, adding some details of my own: 'My mother says this with good intentions – that is, affectionately.' And so on.

Meanwhile, that episode of the mourning period culminated in a family catastrophe that, I realised only two or three years later, could have been avoided, had I not been slavishly exact in transmitting the messages.

The prelude to this episode was our being informed one night in Cairo that my grandfather had died; at dawn on the following day we boarded a train bound for Upper Egypt.

At my grandfather's house the women wailed, my grandmother, my aunt, and some other women I didn't know sitting on the floor despite the seats that lined the walls. I asked my aunt, who explained to me that such were the rites of mourning in our part of the world, and I passed this information along to my mother when she asked. She said, 'But I don't want to sit on the floor!' And with that she seated herself on a chair, crossed her legs, and lit a cigarette!

(I can't omit these details, because they turned up later in the catalogue of my mother's blunders.)

After the sunset prayer, my mother asked my grandmother, 'When will supper be served? We haven't eaten since this morning!' The translation was no sooner out of my mouth than I realised how outrageous this remark was. I could read it in the face of my grandmother, who kept silent.

I turned to my mother and said, 'Perhaps that's the way things are done around here – just like sitting on the floor.'

'Aren't you hungry?'

'No, I'm not hungry.'

'But they aren't poor – why don't they serve supper to their guests? Aren't we guests?'

'We're not guests, Mama – Granny always says to me, "This is your home, Nada, your father's and grandfather's house."'

My grandmother likely told my aunt what the wife of her son had said – whether disapprovingly or with the object of getting her daughter to feed the hungry lady, I don't know. But my aunt leaned over toward my mother and whispered in her ear, so we got up with her, left the house, and set off to a different house.

'It's very odd,' said my mother to my aunt. 'You're not poor, and there are so many guests – you ought to have prepared some food for them, even if it was only sandwiches!'

I translated. My aunt replied, 'Ours is the largest clan in the whole region. At weddings and other big occasions we provide countless animals to be sacrificed for the feasts!'

I asked, 'What does "clan" mean?'

'It means all your kin.'

'What does "kin" mean?'

'Oh, pet, my little niece, you're still a foreigner like your mother. A clan is a family that is thousands strong.'

I translated. But my mother insisted, 'They should have served some food, since they're not poor, or else they should have advised us to bring our own food with us!'

I translated, and my aunt replied, 'Tell her she should be ashamed of herself. It's unthinkable even to talk about food, and your grandfather not yet cold in his grave!'

I translated. My mother got angry, and my aunt changed her mind about taking us to the home of her mother's brother for supper. 'There's no need to make a scene!' she said. I translated.

My mother decided she was not going to stay for the three days of mourning after all, if it meant she and her daughter would have to starve to death. We left at dawn the following day.

My aunt swore that her tongue would never again address a word to her brother's wife, and that she would never set foot in her house for the rest of her life (and she kept this vow). Nor was that the end of the matter, for the grievance was kept alive and it was the first thing my father heard about from his mother, his sister and his cousins when he went to the village after his release. And it was one of the sore points he brought up every time he and my mother quarrelled. During their last row, I told my father it had been my fault. 'I don't believe it,' he said sceptically.

'We left before the three days were up, because of the translation, ya Abu Nada!'

'What translation?' So I told him. He laughed, and made peace with my mother.

Their many rows following his release from detention didn't trouble me, so their decision to separate hit me like a thunderbolt.

Chapter four

Mahariq

M Y FATHER DIDN'T WRITE about his years of detention, nor did he talk about them. Perhaps my interest in prison memoirs – which began with a collection of whatever I could find concerning Wahaat Detention Centre – had its origins in my desire to know the details of my father's life during the five years I lived apart from him: the cell he stayed in, the bed he slept in, the food he ate, the corridor he traversed when he went in or out, the kind of work that was demanded of him, and his relations with his prison-mates and his gaolers. My imagination, where my father was concerned, was restricted by the dearth of memories preceding his arrest, while the period between his arrest and his release is a blank, alleviated only by occasional meetings in a dingy room inside a gloomy building, which we reached after an arduous journey on whose end we congratulated each other when the building loomed before us in the distance, in the bleak pallor of the desert.

For five years, my imagination roamed aimlessly in search of a place to alight. Then, when prison memoirs started to emerge, one after another, I began reading them avidly, filling the gaps in my imagination with solid details, which cut like barbed wire. The newly acquired knowledge, however cruel, helped safeguard me against these gaping holes, erecting a bridge by which it was possible to pass from one level to another and reach that point at which Nada's story and her own personal history was interrupted, and her father was restored to her intact, despite everything.

I could describe Urdy Abu Zab'al with its six wards. I could describe Wahaat Detention Centre with its three wards, number one of which was designated for convicted Communists, number two for detainees such as my father, who hadn't been tried or convicted, and number three for members of the Muslim Brotherhood. I know the location of the ten cells in each ward, of the toilets, and of the officer's room that faces the gate to the ward. My imagination can follow my father at 'Azab Prison in Fayoum, then at Liman Tora, and then for four years at Mahariq Prison in the oases. At this last prison I can put together an image of my father waking up in the morning in one of the ten cells that were in Ward Number Two; I can picture him then going out barefoot into Scorpion Valley carrying a pickaxe for breaking up rock. His attention would be divided between his labour and keeping his eyes and ears alert for any sudden movement or sound betraying a viper that might leap all at once from its lair and deliver its fatal bite. I imagine him when it's time to return to the ward for supper and after that, following evening activities, a cup of tea.

I turn quickly the pages that deal with torture, but take my time reading those that tell of the farm, the theatre, and the mosque, all of which they established in that sea of sand. I contemplate Abdel Azim Anis as he recalls what he taught to students at London University. He would write complex mathematical equations on the floor of the cell, acceding to the wishes of Mohammed Sayyed Ahmed, who wanted to learn. I fix my gaze upon imprisoned doctors who saved the life of the warden's son, and the surgeon who performed an operation with the equipment on hand (and without anaesthetics) for Sergeant Mutawi, who had given orders for torture. I commit the scenes to memory like the stanzas of Fouad Haddad:

> All through the night
> I see the full moon slivered
> I see the full moon slivered behind bars
> I see the full moon slivered behind bars and its night is
>   long.

At school I studied the lines from Imru al-Qays:

> Night like sea waves has dropped its curtains
> Upon me with a multitude of woes to try me.
> So I said to it when, camel-like, it stretched its back,
> Lowered its hindquarters and crouched under its own
>   weight,
> Oh long night, disperse,
> Though daylight be no brighter.

But how was a girl in the first year of senior school to grasp the meaning behind these lines? How could she comprehend this complex imagery of alienation? A cavernous night of afflictions coming one upon the other like sea-waves, it surrounds you; you shoulder its burdens like a she-camel defying gravity, but in vain; you try to find release by looking toward morning, but give up the attempt; night or day, desert

27

or sea, space open or closed, motion or stillness, present or future: no difference, no escape.

Many years later I understood, and when I did, I found myself making a connection between Imru al-Qays's lines and those of his distant descendant, Fouad Haddad:

I don't want dawn to come . . . oh people, I don't want it.
Each time dawn comes, I . . . I, poor anguished soul
Wherever my father kissed me, there they beat me;
Wherever my mother kissed me, there they beat me,
Beatings like insults to your injured womb.
For what did you carry me in your womb, nourish me on
    your food?
For what did you call me by my name – and they call me
By a number written on the skullcap, the mattress, and the
    blanket?
For what, my mother, did we read,
For what did I go to school,
Learn the alphabet?
For what, the books, the indexes, the tests, the Eid gifts?
For what, my mother, did I start out human?
Abdel Latif has inherited your son to be one more of his
    slaves,
Abdel Latif Rushdie is his lord,
Abdel Latif Rushdie is a knight astride the government's
    horse,
With an owl inscribed on his face:
Behind him goes catastrophe, before him a cudgel.

I heard these lines for the first time at university, and I memorised them, although it took years for me to learn their context. Take, for example, this line, which might not be the most eloquent of those selected: 'Abdel Latif Rushdie is a knight astride the government's horse.' We need only infer that Abdel Latif Rushdie is one of the officers who tortured the detainees in order to understand this line. But its meaning is still incomplete, perhaps even deficient, falling far short of a context that infuses the picture with history, facts, agonies: insults and abuse, kickings, starvation and terror. Beatings on the head and face, beatings on the neck and back, beatings on the chest and stomach, the arms and legs, the feet. Beatings with canes, with truncheons, with palm-branches, with leather straps, with shoes. Blows delivered by the hands and kicks by the feet, lashes with whips, flayings. It was 'Do as you're told by the sergeant, you son of a bitch!' 'Say, "I'm a woman," you son of a whore!' and 'Abdel Latif Rushdie is a knight astride the government's horse,' presiding over the action and carrying it out, torturing a line of men being trans-ported to hard labour, their bodies emaciated, faces pale, clothing threadbare, hands ulcerated, feet cracked and swollen with suppurating wounds, descending into a trench to break up basalt under armed guard. 'Abdel Latif Rushdie is a knight astride the government horse.' He tortures Shuhdi Atiyya to the point of death – and he dies.

And Abdel Latif Rushdie, although alone in the poem, brings with him other officers, whose names, traits, words and actions the context supplies for us – the lords and masters of the prison: Major-general Ismail Hemmat, Major Hasan Mounir, Captain Mourgane Ishaq and Second Lieutenant Yunus Mar'i, among others.

Take for example Major Fouad, who led the campaigns for torturing the Muslim Brothers in the Citadel and Abu Za'bal prisons during the 1950s. He looks well settled-in behind his desk, in full uniform, where he directs operations. Abusive obscenities first, then punches and kicks, followed by blind-folding and suspending the prisoner naked, to deliver electric shocks to him and extinguish cigarettes on his body repeatedly, from every side.

Is this major in fact Major-general Fouad, who keeps appearing on the satellite channels with his silver hair and his elegant suit, speaking earnestly and without batting an eye, no tremor in his voice, no twitch in his hands or any part of his face, answering questions addressed to him by the host, who has introduced him as an expert on terrorism and sanctioned organisations?

I talk to Hazem a great deal about my desire to write a book that deals comprehensively with the prison experience. I tell him about each new book I acquire. (I was eager to get my hands on whatever books I could find that addressed this subject. There was a fairly good library available to me that housed biographies of the political prisoners at Mahariq Prison in the oases, the military prison; Citadel and Tora prisons, Abu Za'bal, Istinaf and Qanatir in Cairo; Hadra Prison in Alexandria; and 'Azab Prison in Fayoum. Later I added to it new books on similar experiences at Al-Khiam Detention Centre in southern Lebanon, at Israeli prisons, at Tazmamart in Morocco and Robben Island in South Africa.)

Hazem accuses me of being self-destructive, and says I'm not going to write a book, that I'm merely addicted to reading these accounts, which leave me depressed: 'You'll never write this book!' he says. 'Anyway, it's an impossible task – how could you cover all these experiences in one book?'

Angry with him, I cut him off for a few weeks, and then we meet again for lunch or dinner. I'm hoping he won't reopen the discussion. And at our reconciliation get-together he doesn't broach the subject. But afterward he reverts as usual, and brings it up again, so we quarrel – or not, because I tell him about some of the paradoxes I intend to include in the book. He laughs when I tell him about Abdel Sadiq, the gaoler who, exhausted from the exertion of beating the detainees and showing signs of the onset of a heart attack, began shouting at them, 'You sons of bitches, is there no mercy in your hearts?' And Oukal, who confided to one of the prisoners, in something of an apologetic tone, that he was just the warden's lackey, and only following orders: 'When you get out of here, go into government and give me Abdel Latif Rushdie, and I'll beat *him* . . . give me Gamal Abdel Nasser himself, and I'll beat him, too – I do the government's bidding. I tell you it's happened before your time, and I tell you it'll happen again afterward.'

Or the incident when the prisoners were shaved – their hair, eyebrows and pubes. Hazem says, 'I've heard that one before – everyone's written about it.' 'But I can tell you more. The prisoner who's just been shaved goes back to his ward, more naked than the day his mother gave birth to him, and is surprised when his cellmate looks him up and down and says, "Who are you?" '

I didn't talk to Hazem, or anyone else for that matter, about the mouse incident that was cited in the testimonial of an inmate at Tadmur Prison in Syria. With his own eyes he witnessed another inmate being forced to swallow a dead mouse. I couldn't bear to recall that tale, whether in imagination or in conversation, though it haunted me for weeks, even in my sleep, when it came back to me in nightmares.

31

But I told Hazem about the Spanish woman who wrote about her prison experience during the reign of Franco. 'This woman formed an extraordinary friendship in solitary confinement. She got to be friends with someone whose movements she followed in the cell, and who was her constant companion, observing her and talking to her all the time, telling her about herself and her husband and her three children, who'd been farmed out to three different families, because her husband was also a prisoner.'

'Didn't you say she was in solitary confinement? How could this friend reach her?'

'Guess.'

'Was it a tree?'

'No.'

'A bird?'

'No. I don't remember whether there was any access to the cell. Perhaps the wall had no openings at all.'

'A model she traced on the wall of the cell?'

'No.'

'Then she must have summoned up her friend in her imagination.'

'No.'

'I'm stumped.'

'The friend she loved and depended on was . . . a fly.'

There was a long silence. Finally I broke it. 'I'm going to write a chapter of my book on this woman.'

'Are you going to write about political detention in Egypt, or in the world?'

'I don't know.'

'But you've been saying that you'd drawn up a plan for the book.'

'I have three plans.'

'Good heavens!'

'There's no need for mockery.'

'All right, then let's talk seriously. Plan number one?'

'A book on the experiences of Egyptian prisoners at Mahariq, concluding with a chapter on my father.'

'Dozens of people who've lived through that experience have recorded it – what would you add to their accounts?'

'I don't know.'

'All right, then. Plan number two?'

'An edited volume, each chapter of which contains a selection from the writings of political prisoners from a particular country, Arab or non-Arab. I would edit the book and introduce it with a general study of the subject.'

'And plan number three?'

I faltered a moment. Then I said, 'I forget!'

I hadn't forgotten, but I was embarrassed to talk about my intention to write a novel that would invert the usual order of things, whereby it is those living outside the prison who are the prisoners, not the other way round. The idea was very tempting, but it was just an idea, one that crossed my mind from time to time, and had come to seem like the germ of some sort of literary enterprise. I'm not a novelist, so where did I come up with this mad idea of writing a novel, anyway?

Chapter five

Translation problems II

I N THE BEGINNING, IT was a honeymoon. A resplendent month, it extended spontaneously into the months that followed. The days leading up to it were like wedding celebrations, the house rocked by a feverish commotion of joy – and the guests, the good wishes, the '*Hamdillah 'a-ssalaama*,' 'Thank God you're safe,' 'Your presence illuminates the house' . . . and the chocolates, the sweets, baskets of fruit, flowers, and the potted houseplants delivered by one of the florist's employees, each with a greeting card bearing the name of whoever had sent it.

My grandmother came from the village, bringing stuffed pigeons and ducks, and salted rice pudding. She also brought another gift, entrusted to her by my aunt (for the festivities in no way mitigated against her vow never again to darken the door of her sister-in-law's house). My aunt sent *fiteer* pastry and *meneyn* biscuits, as well as dates and pomegranates. (My mother tasted none of this – she declared that it hadn't been intended for her, and that it wouldn't be right for her to eat any of it.) My father's relatives – cousins on both his father's side and his mother's – brought cartons filled with bags of rice, flour, lentils, sugar, bottles of oil and soap, as well as bottled sherbet. The kitchen filled up with pies, cakes and petits fours, brought by my parents' friends.

My mother went off to work lively, and came home livelier still, buzzing around like a bee, greeting people, bidding them goodbye, welcoming them, hosting them, laying the table, clearing it, all the while lighthearted and smiling. Lately we had engaged the services of a woman – the wife or sister of the *bawaab*, I think, or perhaps it was just someone he knew – to help us around the house. She would stand at the kitchen sink for hours, ceaselessly washing plates and cups, preparing tea and coffee, squeezing lemons and oranges and mixing sherbet with cold water.

I went to school, and when I returned home my feet had wings, as if I was flying to get to Eid. I didn't spend a lot of time staring into the mirror to see what it was that was new about my face. The changes in my mother, though, were perfectly obvious to me. 'Mama,' I said to her, 'you look prettier, and your voice is sweeter, too!' She laughed. I don't think it was her voice that had changed, but rather the cadence of her speech, which in retrospect I believe was smoother, just like the angles of her shoulders, spontaneously restored to their original soft curves. The difference seemed obvious to me on an intuitive level, even if I lacked both the knowledge and experience of people to understand these changes, and the facility to articulate them the way I can do now. My mother's intense vitality – manifested in the swift agility of her movements and complemented by the sweetness of her gaze – had hardened during the period of my father's absence. The lines of her body had grown angular and harsh, as if to express the effort of maintaining her composure and keeping her anxiety in check. But the strain showed in the unevenness

35

of her speech, her high-pitched voice, and the erratic motions of her head and limbs.

After a week or two, the private honeymoon commenced. A sense of calm – pure and fine, novel and altogether strange – united the three of us. My mother and I no longer picked quarrels with each other, she no longer shouted, or spoke or moved in that spasmodic way that had made me think she was mad. In light of these new developments, I concluded that she was not mad after all, that rather she must have been in a bad way, exhausted, and frightened for my father. Or perhaps she had been mad, and was now well again. I began to relax into my life with my parents. Gradually I regained that childhood paradise from which I had fallen abruptly one winter morning, incomprehensibly, unreasonably.

I needed no wings to fly – I could soar even when I was chained to my seat in the classroom. Lessons were enjoyable, the teacher amiable, my classmates the nicest of God's creations. I even approached the one-eyed beggar, who used to stand at the top of the street where my school was, and whose appearance frightened me so that I hurried past him without looking in his direction. I asked him his name, and took to saying, 'Good morning, 'Amm Darwish!' and giving him whatever I could spare – my pocket money if I had remembered to bring any, or the sandwich my mother had made for me, or a piece of chocolate if I happened to have some with me.

Even though I spent a great deal of time sitting with my parents – staying up late with them, fighting sleep until it overcame me and my mother took me off to bed – nevertheless, contrary to both precedent and expectation, at the end of that school year and the next I got the highest marks in every subject we were taught. The day the certificates were distributed, the headmistress announced, 'Nada has distinguished herself in every way; her academic performance is outstanding, likewise her behaviour with the teachers and with her classmates.'

I didn't wait until my father came home. I rang him up at work and then, before he answered, I handed the receiver to my mother, saying, 'You tell him – tell him what the headmistress said!'

What happened after that? Nothing! No earthquake surprised us, no cannon-fire brought the roof down upon the heads it sheltered. Merely foolish little disagreements. I watched, standing by in helpless confusion, as if seated before one of those jigsaw puzzles with hundreds of little pieces, needing to find the right place for every piece in order to complete the picture. Was my father, suffering from some obscure feelings of guilt, in a hurry to establish his position as head of the household? Had the years spent away from us, in oppressive conditions, destroyed his equilibrium, throwing all of us off-balance? Had my mother, after his years away and her own ordeal, expected him to return laden with the flowers of love, understanding and sympathy? Or was misinterpretation at the root of their differences, their mutual intentions lost in translation?

My father was smoking feverishly, and my mother wouldn't stop reminding him that he had quit smoking when she was pregnant with me. She complained of the odour of smoke that pervaded the house (despite the fact that she herself smoked a cigarette or two occasionally). She threw the windows open wide, and he complained of the cold. She complained about some mates of his who would visit him

37

without bringing their wives; he would sequester himself with them, shutting her out, and yet she was expected to provide for them as guests. 'Why didn't you make supper?' 'You didn't say they were going to have supper with us!' At first, with 'please', and a smile, then later 'please', but no smile; thereafter a reproachful frown, and at last matters devolved into a battle, in which other issues got mixed up: 'I don't understand. Your friends show up without any notice, your cousins come and linger forever, and everyone who comes from the village insists on staying with us. What about that thing known as a hotel, which is designed for people to stay in? What's more, these relatives of yours, all the while you were gone, only came for brief visits: ten minutes at most, and off they went!' Perhaps he explained, once or twice, but she didn't understand, and he gave up the attempt. Was he simply exhausted, unequal to the constant translation, or was it that he wished to impose on her his own system, his authority, without endless discussion? He took to saying 'Yes' and 'No' curtly, with no opening for debate. He seemed hard and ungiving, as if we were a heavy weight, an additional burden upon him.

My relationship with him was not like the one I had with my mother, the pattern of which had been set by the life we'd shared on our own, in the absence of our third family member. She would shout, and I would shout back; she would issue orders I would fling back in her face, across the dividing wall. We would quarrel, but at the end of the day find no recourse except to each other in our mutual need – or perhaps we found only our despair, fear and loss, and thus we automatically drew closer to each other, quite as if we hadn't, but a few hours earlier, been at each other's throats like two murderous roosters ready to tear each other to pieces. When my father's return changed everything else, my relationship with my mother remained unchanged. In my battles with my father, on the other hand, no matter how defiant and sure of my own position I was each time I confronted him, he would make me lose my bearings, exhausting me, reducing me to a heap of unrelieved wretchedness.

For five years my father had been an unattainable dream; when he came back, I wanted him to be a dream in whose sanctuary I might live. It may be for this reason that any conflict between us always loomed much larger than the actual problem that had occasioned it, escalating instantly into a crisis that threatened to topple my dream. This made me frantic with anxiety, driving me into a state of panic which the situation didn't in the least call for.

Within two years of my father's release, his troubles with my mother became an open conflict. Three years after our reunion, they had begun, in my presence, to talk about initiating divorce proceedings. I believe it was the issue of those hundred pounds that was the precipitating event – it was, as they say, the straw that broke the camel's back: the 'camel', of course, was our little family, living in a flat comprised of three rooms not one of which was large enough to have accommodated an actual camel.

My mother asked my father about the money that had been kept in a drawer, and he told her he'd given it to his cousin. She didn't understand, so he explained. 'His mother-in-law died in hospital yesterday, and it was clear he was going to need the money.'

'When will he pay you back?'

'I don't expect him to pay me back. In difficult times we help each other out.'

'You should have told him the money was a loan, and specified when it was to be repaid.'

He turned away from her, sending an unmistakable message that he had no wish to continue the discussion. But she persisted, 'You had no right to dispose of that money without consulting me. First of all because it was meant for our family, and secondly because most of it was money I earned from my job. You took money that belonged to me without my knowledge!'

He slapped her.

For a moment the three of us stood there, stunned, and then my father walked out and left the flat. My mother shouted at me, 'Go to your room! What are you doing here, anyway?' I went to my room and slammed the door, thinking, this madwoman can't tell an enemy from a friend – I was on *her* side, and had been on the point of taking her part in an all-out assault on my father, spelling out all of his offences. But she, instead of striking back at him when he hit her, turned on me: 'What are you doing here?' I opened my door and shouted at her, 'What did I do, materialise from Upper Egypt to interfere with your happy life with my father? No, I came because the entire building could hear the two of you fighting!'

But the next day I saw that her eyes were red with weeping, and I wanted to cheer her up. I sat beside her and kissed her. 'Mama,' I said, 'do you think Papa is acting strange?'

'He behaves oddly sometimes. Not like himself.'

'Do you think he lost his mind in prison?'

'No, he hasn't lost his mind. Even though he behaves badly sometimes. Maybe he hasn't adjusted yet to normal life.'

'You claim he's highly intelligent. So how do you explain the stupid things he does?'

'Your father isn't stupid!'

'I think he is!'

'Well I think you're an insolent girl!'

'I'm not insolent – it's just that I'm living with two lunatics! I reckon you're as mad as he is!'

I left her and went into my room, slamming the door behind me. All through my adolescence, this was the registered trademark by which I advertised my wrath.

When they divorced, my mother asked for custody of me. I looked at my father. His face was suffused with a bluish pallor. He said nothing. I asked her, 'Are you staying here or going to France?' She said she would return to France. 'I can't leave my school and my classmates,' I told her. 'I'll stay here with my father.' But I had known to begin with that I wanted to stay with him, even though I wasn't confident that he wanted me (already he didn't want his wife, so did he want her daughter?). I said, 'I'll stay,' even though a few months earlier, when matters between them were heating up, my motto had been, 'They can both go to hell!'

It seems likely that during this period my father, despite all the trouble he had with me and our frequent clashes, put it all down to the intransigence of a wilful child whose mother had never managed to curb her rebelliousness and bring her up properly. And until that memorable visit to Paris in the summer of '68, he retained his ability to restrain my insubordination, never feeling as though I had injured his pride, or intentionally insulted him. Perhaps this was also partly – notwithstanding my slogan, 'They can both go to hell'

– because I put up no resistance to the moments of affection and ease that smoothed over the bad feelings following a row: we would calm down and carry on as before; I would call him 'Abu Nada' and he would refer to me fondly as his 'hazelnut'. We could laugh and joke together, and play word-games. I was happy, too, when he sat and helped me with my maths. I wasn't especially good at maths, yet I was determined to get into the College of Engineering, like him. He said, 'Humanities might be a better match for your abilities.' I didn't take his advice. He began teaching me maths. I understood his explanations, and by practising with them assiduously, I achieved outstanding marks. I was pleased, and so was he.

In those moments of ease we played games with poetry. He would recite a line, and I would have to follow it with a line that began with the same letter with which the previous one had ended. One evening he asked me, 'How many lines of poetry do you know by heart?'

His question took me by surprise. As a matter of pride I said confidently, 'I know lots and lots of lines, Papa – countless lines. Give me two days and I'll have them all for you!' With that 'two days' I was trying to buy myself some time, but I managed to wangle a full week out of the deal by claiming that I had too much homework. I was in fact spending my evenings bent over my desk, but I wasn't doing a single one of my assignments – instead I was reviewing all the poetry I had ever memorised, and learning new poems besides, which I would recite out loud to myself as I lay in bed. I would doze off in the middle of a stanza by Imru al-Qays or Al-Mutanabbi or Shawqi or Al-Jawahiri, or Al-Shabi. It seemed to me that only with my answer could I ransom my image and my father's respect.

At breakfast a week after my father's startling question, I proudly announced, 'I know three hundred lines of poetry by heart, Papa — besides all the French poetry I've memorised, of course!'

At night we would hold our contest. 'Ready?' he said.

'On one condition,' I replied. 'I go first!'

'Agreed!'

In the evening I prepared his tea and sat down opposite him at the square kitchen table. I began.

'Should the people one day yearn for life, then fate to them must yield — *d*.

'Destiny with grievous losses has assailed me, until its arrows do my heart engulf — *f*.

'Forbid not that which you do yourself, for in so doing lies great shame — *e*.

'Each man may not achieve what he hopes for, to the will of ships do winds contrary blow — *w*.

'*W* . . . *w* . . . *w* . . .'

'Hazelnut, your minute's up — you lose one point!'

'My minute's not up!'

'Yes, it is. *W*, if you please, Lady Hazelnut:

We make ready the sword and lance, but death slays us without a fight — *t*.'

'The flanks of a gazelle has he, the legs of an ostrich . . .'

He interrupted me before I could finish the line. 'Choose another line — that one begins and ends with a *t*. It won't do.'

'Why won't it do?'

'That's one of the rules of the game. You're not allowed to use a line that begins and ends with the same letter. Find another line.'

43

But my memory refused to come up with another line that started with *t*.

I stalled. 'I need to go to the toilet.'

'Say the line and then go.'

'Papa, I can't – I have to go to the toilet *now*!'

I went to the toilet, closed the door, and tried to think of a line that started with the letter *t*. Then I went back to the kitchen. 'I can't think of a line that starts with *t*! Papa, it's not fair – I really did need to go to the toilet!'

He laughed uproariously. I joined in.

'Two points,' he said. Next:

'Then he took refuge behind a rock on Radwa summit, among the soaring peaks of mountains high – *h*.'

I tried to remember a line that started with the letter *h*, but I couldn't.

'Three points – you're out, Hazelnut!' Then:

'Heroic in magnanimity the branching limb, that bends as need requires but will not break.'

He usually won. All the same, though, I enjoyed it every time we competed, because I loved playing games with him, and I loved listening to him recite poetry – the timbre of his voice, his enunciation of the letters, his style of delivery all enchanted me. When he declaimed a line I had trouble understanding, I would say, 'Explain,' and he would explain, and I would take still more pleasure in the meanings of the passages as he elucidated them for me.

In the spring of 1968, when I was fourteen, my father introduced me to a woman I hated on sight. When he asked me what I thought of her, I launched straight in with my criticism of her looks, her height, her girth, the clothes she wore, her hairstyle, and the way she spoke. He tried to argue with me, to sway me by enumerating her virtues, which only increased my dislike for her. I said, 'So why does she slather her face with loads of makeup, like some bit-player in a Farid al-Atrash film, all ready to dance in the background as soon as the music begins?

He didn't laugh, and I was bewildered – I had assumed he would be as amused as I was by the impromptu comparison with which I had surprised even myself.

A few weeks later he started talking to me about her again. I said, 'Who, the bit-player?'

He got angry then, and left the room. He didn't speak of her again to me.

When examinations were over, I went to France to meet my mother in Paris, as I had promised her I would do, and to spend the summer holidays with her.

It would be the first time we saw each other since she had left Cairo nine months earlier. When she spread her arms wide to embrace me I was surprised to discover how much I had missed her, and I was the more puzzled that in Cairo I had been unaware of these feelings – of how attached to her I was and how much I needed her; it was as if I had decided all at once to fasten a belt, like in an aeroplane. Perhaps that surrender to my need for my mother was a luxury I couldn't afford. Her departure had seemed a matter of course. I suffered under the strain of accepting that swift collapse of the status quo, although indifference was still the predominant attitude I affected in my behaviour and emotions (such emotions as I admitted to, that is).

When I saw her at the airport I was startled by the tumbling of those walls I hadn't, to begin with, even realised I had erected and retreated behind. I held on to her for a long time, hugging her tightly, and on our way out of the airport I held her hand just the way I had used to do as a child, clinging so hard I was practically digging my nails into her palm. This time she didn't object.

At the supper table at home, I was struck by something else. I had noticed it at the airport, but it hadn't given me pause then, for I had been too taken up with the pleasure of seeing my mother, and too preoccupied with my own unexpected reactions and feelings. Or perhaps in that moment I had assumed it was simply that she was so moved by the sight of me after nine months of separation. Certainly I had noticed her pallor, even as I was walking toward her with my bag on the luggage trolley – I saw it from a distance, before I reached and embraced her. But now, as she sat opposite me while we had our supper, I looked at her more closely. Her face was still pale, and this wasn't the only thing about her that was new. What else? Was it possible that old age could overtake someone who was only forty-five? And could this happen in just nine months?

'Mama, are you ill?' She said she was not. I asked her whether she had been ill in the preceding months. She assured me that she hadn't.

'Mama, your face is pale. It wasn't like that in Cairo – even on the day you left it wasn't this pale!'

She laughed, and changed the subject. 'Today it's forbidden to talk about our troubles – we're celebrating our reunion.'

Once I was alone in bed, I didn't sleep – I didn't drift off even for a few minutes. I was mulling over those two unexpected developments, trying to understand. wondering and wondering – what was happening?

I started with the second thing, which in reality was fore-most: my mother's condition. What was it about her that was new? It wasn't merely that pallor – so what was it, then? Something different about the look in her eye? (A sadness mingled with a questioning expression – or something else, too difficult for me to read?) A slowness, unlike before, in the movement of her body and her hands? She was a beautiful woman. There was in her face a sweetness arising not only from the fineness and harmony of her features, but also from the spark in the honey-coloured eyes that were the first thing about her to catch your attention. Intelligence shone from them – reminding you of nothing so much as the gleam in a mischievous child's eye – lending a certain vividness to her face the moment she opened her mouth to speak. She had a nervous energy that ebbed and flowed, imparting to her rather petite body an animation that expressed itself in the cadences of her speech and the rapidity of her movements. Did she seem changed because her hair was a different length? She had used to keep her hair short, barely even reaching her neck, with a fringe in front. Now it had grown long, extending down her back, and she had tied it in a ponytail. With the ponytail she looked more like me, for I have the same facial features as she, although I have my father's dark eyes and his height. But this was not the time for sorting out the question of what traits I'd inherited from whom. Was she ill? She struck me as brittle, brittle in the way of someone defeated; or, to put it another way, it was as if liveliness had given way to something softer, as if something in her (that nervous energy, or animation) had receded, or been stilled or extin-guished. Was it the loneliness of living by herself in a strange country? But she was French, so how could France be a

47

strange country? Did she find herself a foreigner there after all those years in another country? Was she worn out by her daily toil? Did she miss my father? Did she want to go back to Cairo?

These questions started me out on a path I had never before approached, or even conceived of, a dim awareness that began right away, but gradually, to form itself as an impression that she might need my care and protection. Perhaps I ought not to leave her alone. I had never really thought about how much I depended on her. A little girl depends on her mother without giving it a thought. I was surprised by my longing for her — a longing so strange I could scarcely believe it. How could there be such longing if I was insensible to it while I was far from her? She wrote me lengthy letters, to which I replied with two or three words, as if out of a sense of duty rather than genuine feeling. She pressed me to write to her, and I would chafe at her insistence, going weeks without writing at all. Why then, when I saw her — from the first moment I saw her — was I engulfed by this flood of yearning and tenderness, and the desire to cling to her and weep, and tell her it was all a mistake, a huge mistake? The word buzzed in my ear while we were at the airport, and I didn't know what I meant by it: her breakup with my father? Her going back to France? My not having gone with her? I had no answer to any of this, and all that night I stayed awake turning the riddles over in my mind, but could come up with no satisfactory solutions; I might seem to find one, but none I could settle on for longer than a few minutes before returning once more to the inquiry.

What happened in Paris is that I encountered the truth of my feelings toward my mother and from there I automatically followed – in a way I didn't comprehend at the time – the trajectory of my perception that she was in need of protection. Now it was for me to learn, gradually, how to open my arms to embrace and protect, to relax my guard and show compassion, to undertake the role of mother to my own mother. Why then did I not follow through? I forgot, or pretended to forget. Or such is life, that it takes us out of our feelings, or it withdraws those feelings and sets them far from our intentions.

Also in Paris that summer, I made my first step toward taking an interest in public events. In childhood, my father's arrest was an entirely personal event, no more than that: a reasonless, incomprehensible removal to an obscure place. After my father's release, politics were not, at home, a matter of daily discourse in which all three of us engaged at meals or in our evenings spent together as a family. Even the 1967 'setback', which I followed to some extent, didn't – as far as I can recall – penetrate the fabric of my emotional life until later, retrospectively. In June of 1967 I was beginning senior school, following the news of the war and the defeat in radio broadcasts, newspapers, and what I heard repeated, indirectly, allusively, on the tongues of others. But the event in all its tragic import did not permeate the inner life of a thirteen-year-old girl preoccupied with her relationship with her father, and his relationship with her mother, and with the upheavals of a family in a painful process of disintegration, the fear of a dissolution that seemed imminent.

(It was the night Nasser revealed, in the course of his speech announcing the defeat, his intention to step aside – a dark night. My father was following the speech and brushing away tears with the back of his hand. He went on brushing them

49

and brushing them. My consternation at tears shed by my father was greater than anything occasioned by the nation's president reporting a rout whose impact I would not absorb until years afterward – that is, I would absorb it more fully with the passage of years, as a gradual process beginning that day, and perhaps continuing even up to this moment.

The speech ends. My father weeps, wailing like a child. My mother all at once becomes hysterical, shouting, 'I don't understand! I absolutely do not understand! Why are you crying over him? Isn't he the fascist officer, the brutal dictator who put the lot of you in prison for five years without the slightest grounds? Isn't he . . . wasn't he . . . didn't you say . . .?' Her words tumbled out in a rush, her voice pitched higher and higher. Suddenly my father said, 'You must be blind!' Then he walked out – left the house. After that she spoke not a word, and neither did I.)

Chapter six

Paris 1968

W HEN I GOT TO Paris, I hadn't the least idea what the country had witnessed in the previous weeks. But Paris that summer talked of nothing but those events. My mother, the neighbours, acquaintances – all were talking about them, while the newspapers revisited, analysed, and followed up on developments. As the boys and girls I got to know – who were of my own age, or older by a couple of years or so – strove to offer their own interpretations of what had happened, they found it entertaining to pass along the details of those weeks to a girl who had come from the faraway land of Egypt, ignorant of the fascinating things they knew.

My mother introduced me to Gérard and his family, who lived in the same building. The first time we met, Gérard volunteered to accompany me on a visit to any of the city's landmarks I might care to see. I said I wanted to visit Notre Dame (it wasn't that I was interested in church architecture, but I wanted to see the cathedral and its great bell, which the hunchback Quasimodo had rung in the novel by Hugo that I had loved, and that had made me cry). We agreed that he would take me there in two days' time.

Gérard came by for me at ten in the morning; my mother had gone to work. We set off from the house toward Notre Dame. On the way to the Metro, and in the train, Gérard told me about the student demonstrations that had begun on 22 March in Nanterre. Eight students had stormed the dean's office, to protest the arrest of six of their classmates for being active on a committee organised against the Vietnam War. It had been decided that these eight students would come before the disciplinary board a month later.

Gérard said, 'On Friday the third of May, in the forecourt of the university, a group of student activists made a circle around the eight students who were to stand before the disciplinary board the following Monday. The crowd got bigger, and just kept growing. At four o'clock in the afternoon, riot police surrounded the university and began arresting students. As the news spread, even more students began showing up, and a battle ensued between them and the police. The closure of the university was announced – it's only the second time in seven hundred years that the Sorbonne has been closed down; the first time was in 1940, when Paris was occupied by the Nazis.

'Less than ten days after the decision to close the university, the President of the Republic was forced to make the decision to withdraw the police and reopen it. But things were not about to go back to the way they'd been before. The students took over the university. They opened up the gates, so that anyone who wanted to could join them in brainstorming and discussion sessions.

'Between the closure and reopening of the university, lots of battles were waged, and workers' strikes mounted and spread throughout France.'

'Are you sure you want to go to Notre Dame?'

We changed direction.

Gérard took me to the Sorbonne University courtyard. 'Here,' he said, 'with us standing in the courtyard, is where the demonstrations of Friday the third of May took place. From here, on Monday the sixth of May, the eight students marched, singing the National Anthem; they passed through the ring of policemen encircling the campus on their way to the disciplinary hearing. The demonstration heated up and spread into other parts of Paris. While the procession was making its way back into the Latin Quarter, the police attacked it. So the demonstrators began throwing stones they picked up from the street, overturning cars and erecting barricades. Heated clashes ensued, and these were repeated in the days that followed. It wasn't only the students who were setting up barricades, but the residents of the neighbourhood as well; workers, housewives, and passersby all pitched in, supplying stones, planks of wood, rubbish bins, and iron bars. The battles raged all through the night, and house-raids went on all night, too. The police would raid a house and set upon the person they were after with their cudgels and beat him, then carry him out by force and throw him into one of their cars, then move on to the next address.'

We stood in front of the university buildings, which were tranquil now, but in my imagination, and in Gérard's words, they were crowded with demonstrators and police, vivid with slogans and banners.

'I'll show you where traces of the battles can still be seen.'

We headed toward Rue Gay-Lussac.

Gérard went on at length, as we walked along the boulevard, and in the succeeding days, telling me about the battles

53

that had taken place in this street on 'Bloody Monday'. He would talk about the violence of the police, the students' resistance, how many were wounded on both sides, and how many arrested. I would see with my own eyes some of the slogans scrawled on the walls: 'Let our comrades go!' 'Down with the police state!' 'Down with capitalist society!' 'Long live the workers' assemblies!' Out of the dozens of slogans, there were three, written in heavy black marker on the walls of one of the buildings, that would bring me to a halt. One of them said: 'Be realistic – demand the impossible!' The second: 'Let us form committees for dreams!' The third: 'When they test you, answer with questions!' (Later I would write them on the walls of my room in Cairo, and beside them I would hang the two posters Gérard gave me.) Also in rue Gay-Lussac I could see the shredded remains of posters, or spread-open pages from the newspapers, impossible to read because of the plethora of comments appended to them in red, green, and blue ink, in the margins and between the lines; I also noted that parts of the street had been picked clean of stones.

Gérard continued his story, moving from Nanterre to Paris and from Paris to Nantes, then returning to Paris, and from there to the Renault factories at Billancourt. He told me, 'The students said . . .' 'The workers said . . .' 'The students did this . . .' 'The workers did that . . .' I paid close attention, but when the moment came for me to ask questions, I was so afraid of sounding stupid that I held back.

I didn't notice that we had been walking for hours on end until Gérard said, 'It's four o'clock – aren't you hungry? I'm really thirsty.'

We took a road that delivered us to a broad avenue called rue des Ecoles. (I liked the name, and years later, on subsequent visits to Paris, I would be intent on staying in one of the hotels on this street, because I liked the name and because the memory of that day had stayed with me, recalling that nice boy I liked so much, who had conducted me of his own accord to a realm of knowledge that would change many things in my life, at least for some years to come.)

In the rue des Ecoles, we sat in a café and ordered juice and sandwiches.

I went home to my mother flying high, full of stories and questions. I questioned her, and she filled me in on some of the details, telling me where she had been, what she had heard, and what she had done. (I was surprised to learn that she had taken part in the strike.) I asked her about all those points on which I had wanted to question Gérard, but refrained, for fear of appearing ignorant in his eyes: the locations of certain streets and squares, certain people, and letters I knew were initials standing for the names of organisations or guilds or societies, but I didn't know what they meant or what they represented. I asked, she replied, and then she brought me a map of Paris and pointed out places. 'This is the river,' she said, 'and here's the Place de la République, where the main part of the demonstration started out, on Monday the thirteenth of May. And here, on the other side of the river, is the Latin Quarter. This is the Sorbonne' – with her finger she pointed to the location of the university, to the west of the Latin Quarter. She moved her finger farther, then stopped and said, 'Here at the southeastern edge is the Censier Centre, the new building of the University College of Humanities, where the pamphlets were prepared and printed. And this is rue des Ecoles, where you were.'

When I told her 'good night', she kissed me with a smile that seemed somehow odd to me, saying, 'You've grown up, Nada, and – lo and behold – you're interested in politics!' She didn't say 'like your father', but I now believe that the way she smiled had something to do with the words that would have completed her sentence. I finished the sentence for myself years afterward, when she told me that, not quite two decades before the summer of 1968, she had accompanied my father, recently arrived in the city, through the streets of Paris, in order to show him places connected with the soldiers of the German occupation and with the French resistance; and that, some weeks before our reunion, she herself had taken part in the momentous events of Paris.

At the time I didn't understand my mother's smile, and the only part of what she said that struck me was that I had become interested in politics, since it hadn't occurred to me, as I listened to Gérard's fascinating stories, that he was talking about politics. Despite what I heard that day, and over successive days, of battles, and of people injured and killed and arrested, of house raids, of truncheons, tear-gas, smoke bombs, stones, and barricades, the events seemed more like an exciting film than reality.

Two months into my stay in Paris, I knew to the day and the hour the details of the events of May, the student demonstrations, the street battles, the strikes by the workers at the Renault factory and other industrial sites, the positions of the guilds and the workers' unions, what was said and done by the president of the university, the Minister of Education, the Minister of the Interior, and the municipal chief of police. It was as if I was a diligent student registered in an intensive academic programme, deriving from it the utmost possible benefit.

I had Gérard to thank for this, my first friend, and perhaps the first young man I became fond of, without realising that this fondness was known as 'love'. Maybe after all it wasn't love, but interest and admiration that came close to bedazzlement. I wanted to be with him, I looked forward to it, and I prepared for it; then when we were together I didn't notice the time passing. He was a tall and slender young man, with rather coarse hair – or maybe it seemed coarse because he left it unkempt. He generally wore the same trousers and jacket, and a pair of athletic shoes. He was seventeen, or thereabouts. I said to him, 'In two months I'll be sixteen.' (I lied, so that he wouldn't think of me as much younger than he was.) I remember the places where he brought me, I remember the sound of his voice. I remember him telling his story, but I no longer remember his face in any detail, perhaps because I was too shy to look him in the eye or to keep gazing at him while he was talking. My glances at him were always furtive, as if stolen.

Everything Gérard told me was exciting – it stimulated my imagination. The most inspiring scenario of all was his account of what happened at the university after the takeover. The university gates were wide open to whoever might wish to enter. There were heavily attended lectures reviewing consumer society, organised resistance, self-governance, repression, imperialism, ideology and the tactics of disinformation. And in the large auditorium every night, thousands gathered to assess the events of the day and their performance. The dimly-lit corridors of the ancient building were suddenly illuminated with colours and posters and slogans. A photographic exhibition on the night of the barricades. Groups like a beehive whose every cell was busy working on an assignment, gathering its materials and researching the details, one group working on police brutality, a second studying an alternative to the examination system, a third looking into academic freedom, and a fourth, a fifth, a sixth . . . In the university courtyard, where the banners flutter and the young people gather in a circle for discussion and to exchange the writings and pamphlets of their organisations, a piano suddenly appears, on which anyone who wishes and who knows how to play may take a turn.

At our last meeting Gérard gave me a precious gift, which I would bring back with me to Cairo exulting in its value and in the awareness of what it had meant for Gérard to have given up, for my sake, not just one, but two of the posters in his collection. (It was clear when he showed them to me how much he prized them and how proud he felt of having acquired them.) The first poster showed the head of a youth drawn against a black background, with only his eyes visible – wide-open, anxious eyes in a face entirely swathed in bandages from the crown of his head to his neck. Where his mouth should have been a safety pin secured the bandages. The second poster had a white background, and at the top were the words 'The System', and at the bottom the rest of the sentence, 'is safe and sound'; in the space between, halfway down, were two figures drawn in black ink at opposite edges of the poster, carrying between them a stretcher as long as the poster was wide, on which was a person covered by a sheet, dying or already dead.

When we said goodbye, Gérard told me, 'Nada, I'm very happy to have got to know you. If your mother hadn't told me that the prevailing custom in your country is completely different from the way things are done here, maybe we could have been friends in another way.' Then he laughed, 'I've violated one of the basic tenets of the Movement: "Nothing is prohibited except prohibition itself!" But your mother assured me that could completely spoil the relationship, and do real damage.'

I don't know whether I took out on my mother how upset I was at saying goodbye to Gérard, or how intensely moved I was by his gift, or whether it was in order to make it easier to leave her that I picked a quarrel with her. The moment I walked in the house and saw her I said, 'What right did you have to say what you said to Gérard? How dare you tell him anything on my account without consulting me? How dare you interfere in my relationships with my friends?'

She replied with a strange calm, as if she was insensible to the magnitude of my anger and of the problem she had caused, 'You're only fourteen. That warning was necessary, because the way of life here is different, and especially with this generation of young people it's totally different. He might have . . .' I walked out on her before she could finish her sentence. I went into my bedroom and slammed the door.

How dare she appoint herself as my agent? If she hadn't said what she said, maybe Gérard would have told me he cared for me, that he considered me beautiful, that he was wretched at the prospect of my departure. Maybe he would have liked to take my hand and squeeze it, maybe he would have liked to kiss me. He hadn't even tried to kiss me on the forehead. No doubt this madwoman had told him our customs didn't allow it!

My anger imposed itself on our parting the following morning. I said goodbye to my mother coldly, and when she tried to hug me I ducked out of her embrace. I said a curt, dry '*Au revoir*' and I didn't smile. Then I turned my back on her and walked away.

Chapter seven

Back to Cairo

M Y ANGER WITH MY mother didn't last long, perhaps because I received from Gérard a long letter, very kind and sweet, and from my mother I got a letter in which she apologised to me, saying that she hadn't meant to hurt me, or to interfere in my business, and that she knew I was now a young woman who 'understood something of politics', and could make her own decisions. She repeated, 'I'm sorry, Sweetheart.'

The two letters imparted to me a calm that allowed me to contemplate the spoils with which I had returned from my trip to Paris for their own sake, despite the unfortunate incident of the night before my departure: the discovery of the concern I felt for my mother, and my intense need of her. Then, too, I was preoccupied with parading my new knowledge before my friends and – more to the point – my father. I would talk at length about how the students raised their red and black banners over the Arc de Triomphe at the heart of Paris; how they took over the university, the College of Fine Arts, and the Odeon Theatre; how they connected with the workers; how the workers went on strike and work came to a stop at the plants and factories; how the transport workers,

61

by striking, were able to bring to a halt Paris's ground transportation system, and then the trains that connected Paris to other cities. I repeated, 'Nine million went on strike – can you imagine?' I would say this with pride, as if I myself had taken part in organising the strike, or even as if I had been one of its leaders. Carried away by my own enthusiasm, I would move on from there to an attack on the enemy: 'Paul de Roche, he's the one who . . .' And, 'Fouché declared . . .' And 'Gremeau said . . .'

He interrupted me. 'Hold on, Hazelnut, hold on! Who is this de Roche? And who's Fouché? And the other one, the third name you mentioned – who's that?'

I puffed up like a turkey. 'What's the matter with you?' I said. 'Don't you keep up with the news, Abu Nada?'

One evening after dinner, a week after I received my mother's letter, I said to my father, 'Papa, I think Mama's not well. She's pale, and seems exhausted.'

'Is she ill?'

'She told me she wasn't.'

Then I went on, 'Papa, do you know, Mama participated in the May 13th demonstrations!'

'I'm not surprised. She has anarchist leanings.'

I passed over what he'd just said, because I didn't understand it. 'Papa, why not have Mama come back? Couldn't you reverse the divorce?'

He didn't answer. I went on. 'A divorce can be reversed, can't it? If you're with me, let's write to her about it, or ring her up – she'll agree. Or, if she doesn't agree at first, we can just ring her again, maybe a couple of times, and she'll come round.'

'Nada,' he said, 'it's over. We had our differences, and we split up, unfortunately.'

'But since you say it's "unfortunate", can't we still repair the relationship?'

'I don't think so.'

'Why not?'

'Because it ended.'

'Nothing ends!' (Where did I come by this bit of wisdom?)

'I've got involved with another woman, and I'm seriously considering marrying her.'

I shouted, 'Don't tell me it's that second-rate actress!'

'I told you, she is a respectable woman – stop acting like a child!'

The only answer I could come up with was, 'By the way, Papa, the position the French Communist Party took on the student revolution was rubbish. Even the poet Aragon – you know how well-loved he is – when he got up on stage to address the students, they made fun of him, jeering at him, "Long live Stalinism!" And at the May 13th demonstration the position of the workers' union controlled by the Communists was a scandal. They played a suspicious part in the breaking up of the demonstration, and . . .'

He interrupted me. 'The whole movement was nothing but a tempest in a teapot, stirred up with no thought for the consequences. All too often this kind of thing is fomented by the adventurers of a parasitic leftist movement: Maoists, Trotskyites, anarchists.'

I was caught off-guard by the list of technical terms he deployed. What did 'parasitic leftist movement' mean? What was wrong with some of them being Trotskyites? What did 'Trotskyite' mean, anyway? And did the word 'anarchist' have a political meaning, or only its literal one? Was it connected in any way with Gérard's messy hair? And how

could my mother be an anarchist, when she was so scrupu-
lously careful about the arrangement of her clothes and her
house? She had used to scold us for the disorder we created in
the house. What did 'anarchist' mean?

I seized upon the word I knew. 'It's not true – they weren't
adventurers!'

'Oh, yes they were.'

'That's what the French Communist Party said, and it was
a poor position. The young people in the movement in
France are contemptuous of it, and don't have confidence in
the trade-union leadership that subscribes to it. And here I
don't think anyone even knows anything about the
Communists – or cares about them!'

Thrust and parry.

The round was over. I calmed down. Or it seemed to me
that I was calmer. As soon as I was by myself, I confronted the
question: What was I to do if my father married that woman?

Move to Paris and live with my mother?

Move to Upper Egypt and live with my aunt?

What about school?

There was no French school in the village.

I could switch to an Arabic school.

I could stay in Cairo, enrol in a boarding school, and never
have to see that woman's face, slathered with makeup.

The following morning, instead of 'Good morning', I
announced, 'I won't stay in this house if that bit-player comes
to live with us here.'

He shouted at me, 'You spoiled brat, you think of nothing
but yourself! On top of it you're insolent, you don't know
when to give it a rest – no manners, no respect for your elders!
I will marry Hamdiya!' (Oh, my God, and her name's

Hamdiya! I'd forgotten she had a name. Where did her family come up with a name like that?) He said, 'I'll marry her and you'll live with her and you'll treat her with all possible respect. I absolutely will not put up with any of your cheek.'

I shouted at him, 'My mother waits five years for you, while you're in prison, and when you get out you leave her and marry a monkey named Hamdiya!'

He slapped me.

I didn't go to school. I spent the whole day crying. If my mother had been with me she would have known that this crying jag was the longest (longer than the bout of tears over the baby's spitting up on the new red dress I had wanted to dazzle my father with the first time we visited him in prison).

That evening he tried to make up with me, but I refused. For two weeks I didn't say a word to him.

This was the beginning of the most difficult phase of my life. A woman I couldn't stand came to our home to live with us, leaving me nothing of my familiar abode except my bedroom, the only place in the house that was off-limits to her. Her presence in the house made me feel stifled, as if she were not merely treading upon one of my limbs, but actually standing on my chest with all her considerable weight. I wished she would die. Every day, every hour, every moment I wished she would die. The resentment I felt for my father was limitless. He didn't care, paid no attention. He saw nothing, heard nothing, felt nothing. Meanwhile, I crouched with my head in my arms, in a futile attempt to protect it from the debris from the house, some of whose rubble was still coming down on me, wood, glass, and stone, wounding me and causing me to bleed.

It seemed to me that I hated him. It seemed to me that I pitied him, my pity mixed with contempt. I felt my father was stupid – foolish and selfish, that his selfishness was tragic.

I began writing long letters to my mother, and counting the days until hers arrived. I distanced myself from my friends, since it seemed to me that intimacy was not possible unless I talked about my troubles, and I couldn't bring myself to talk about my father in the unfavourable terms in which I had come to view him.

Chapter eight

Ticket to France

WHEN I STARTED ATTENDING secondary school, I read a great deal, but after the bit-player came to live with us I began to read ravenously, ceaselessly. I read novels, books on history, sociology, and politics. (My mother sent me a book on the revolution of '68, which I started reading the moment I received it on my arrival home from school, and I finished it half an hour before school began the next morning; I fell asleep twice in class that day.) I read everything I could get my hands on. Novels were my genre of choice – the use of language enchanted me, its magical power to transport me from here to there, into other times and places, into the lives and destinies of different characters. I laughed and cried, my heartbeat would quicken or seem about to stop altogether, from fear or anticipation of some exciting turn of the plot. I was living a parallel life that absorbed me entirely, far away from Hamdiya and her husband, a life whose settings and casts of characters changed with each new literary work. I would finish one novel and start another, and, as soon as I was done with that one, take up a third. I polished off all the novels in the house that my mother had left behind, or that my father had acquired. Nineteenth-century French novels, whether romantic or realist: works by Hugo, Chateaubriand, Balzac, Stendhal, Flaubert and Zola; Arabic novels by Tawfik al-Hakim, Naguib Mahfouz, and Abdel Rahman al-Sharqawi; Algerian novels written in French by Kateb Yacine and Mohammed Dib; and English novels translated into French or Arabic, by Dickens and the Brontë sisters, Charlotte and Emily. Television was of no interest to me, nor did I play any sports, other than in physical education classes and the required activities in which we had to participate two days a week at the end of the school day.

By the time I was sixteen, my accumulated knowledge was a startling mixture, in which Balzac's peasants mingled with Al-Sharqawi's; the back streets of Cairo crisscrossed with the alleyways of London; to get from Madame Bovary to Amina, the wife of Ahmed al-Sayyed Abdel Gawwad in Mahfouz's trilogy, required no more than a slight turn of the head; and lovesick Heathcliff and Rochester's mad wife, whom he imprisoned in his attic, seemed more real and present to me than the actual human beings with whom I interacted every day. Moreover, all this reading gave me power over my peers. I knew more than they did, so I spoke with ease and confidence – who, after all, at the age of sixteen, could have lived through a protracted, tempestuous love such as Heathcliff's, in which love combined with hatred and evil? To whom was granted the singular experience of transforming in the blink of an eye from the denizen of a thieves' lair in a gloomy city to a splendid young man taking part in a rally in joyful celebration of Saad Zaghloul's return, only to be shot by one of the occupying soldiers? And who, in dreams at night, merged the image of this youth with that of another, his hair unkempt, talking of how he participated in the takeover of the Sorbonne?

In the third year of secondary school my teacher said to me, 'Nada, you have a distinctive style – a subtle, literary style. Will you enrol in the College of Humanities?'

'No,' I replied, 'I intend to join the College of Engineering.'

In the autumn of 1971 I enrolled at the College of Engineering, and by the end of that school year I had failed. It wasn't because I had discovered that the curriculum was dull and I didn't like it or want to continue specialising in it, although in fact I did make this discovery. And it wasn't because of the stress of Hamdiya's being with us at home, for I ignored her completely. I had been preoccupied with student activism. It wasn't merely a matter of participation, but of active involvement in innumerable details and new ideas, and unexpected new horizons that had opened up before me. A new feverishness swept me up entirely, and entwined with it was an attachment to one of my comrades – an attachment that was rather like the roller coaster at an amusement park, carrying me up to dizzying heights and dropping down all at once, only to scale the heights once again.

At the university I buzzed around like a honeybee. I flew from the Engineering School to the Humanities, from Humanities to Economics, then dashed back to Engineering, and finally to the main campus. I attended conferences and council meetings and discussion groups, acceding and dissenting, agreeing and disagreeing, and saying, 'Point of order.' Surprisingly quickly, I became conversant with history and politics, and acquired a lexicon of terms that, a year earlier, I would have thought arcane and inaccessible. At home I copied out communiqués on the typewriter and edited a wall newspaper in which I transcribed articles given to me by my comrades, and then filled any remaining spaces with satirical cartoons, decorations, and lines of poetry both colloquial and formal.

Three months after I started at university, Hamdiya, startled, observed that I was securing the waistband of my trousers with a rope. I explained, 'I seem to have lost a lot of weight. I tried Papa's belt, but found that it was too big.'

'Take off the trousers and put on a dress.'

I didn't answer. I didn't have a clean dress. I pulled my shirt-tail out of my trousers and let it hang down so as to cover my waist and the rope tied around it.

'Okay?'

'Okay,' said Hamdiya. Then, 'Wait a moment.'

She brought a measuring tape and put it round my waist. 'Leave your trousers with me – I'll take them in for you.' By the evening of the following day, I found the three pairs of trousers I'd given her on a hanger suspended from my bedroom door. They'd been washed and pressed. I tried one of them on, and it fitted just right.

The episode of the trousers was nicer than that of Shazli's appearance on the scene.

An amazing paradox: Hamdiya didn't enter my room that day (nor had she ever done so before, of course, since for her it had been a restricted area from the time she moved in). She left the trousers hanging on the doorknob; the door was closed. But that tentative step she took marked a turning point between two phases. Afterwards the door would be opened to her and she would enter quietly, by degrees. I didn't take note of exactly when I first said 'Come in', but I did say it.

Shazli, on the other hand, arrived with an uproar and departed with an even bigger one, leaving behind him a state of chaos, despair, confusion, and a period of years dedicated to my attempt to reassemble the fragments of my life and put it back in order.

Yes, there were two paradoxes; or you might say it was one that consisted, as is usual with a paradox, of two parts.

Shazli came on the scene just the way Hamdiya had, unexpected and unwelcome.

'Is it true you're the daughter of Dr Abdel Qadir Selim?'

'I'd love to meet your father!'

'I want to ask him his opinion on the dissolution of the party, and what his position is on two of his colleagues' having agreed to serve in the ministry, and . . .'

'Your mother is French, isn't she?'

'I heard she knows Aragon, and that she introduced your father to him. I read the interview your father conducted with him in the early 1950s.'

'Could I have a talk with your mother about her memories of Aragon?'

I surprised myself with my answer.

'She wouldn't agree. She's writing her memoir, and it's certain she'll include in it the story of her acquaintance with Aragon.'

His brashness annoyed me – it seemed to me there was more than a little arrogance in his self-assertion. I concocted the notion of a memoir in order to put an end to the discussion.

What can have happened after that, to make me warm up to him and befriend him? A few days later he told me he cared for me, and that maybe I didn't reciprocate the feeling because he was of peasant stock, or because he was dark-skinned with coarse hair – maybe also because his name was Shazli. I laughed at that fourth reason he cited; the remainder of the list was as provocative as the first part: 'And of course you're half French, with smooth hair, the daughter of well-known people, and your name is Nada!' I didn't laugh at his reference to my name; his words felt hurtful. Was he blackmailing me?

At any rate, Shazli succeeded. It was as if he had in some way held out his hand to me, and after I rejected it I became confused, wondering whether he saw in me things I didn't see in myself.

We started seeing each other.

When at last I invited him to come visit us, my father commented on him unfavourably: 'The boy looks like a fish – what do you see in him?'

'He's courageous, shrewd, perceptive, and easygoing, and he understands the common cause.'

' "Shrewd" – do you know the meaning of the word? Look it up in the dictionary!'

'I'll do no such thing! You don't know him. He's my good friend and I know him well!'

I repeated angrily to my father what Shazli had said to me when we were first getting acquainted – repeated it exactly: 'You snub him because he comes from peasant stock, he's dark-skinned, and his name is . . .' And so forth.

'Right,' my father replied sardonically, 'like I'm the Prince of Wales.'

My friendship with Shazli grew stronger during the sit-in. We stuck together in the hall, with thousands of other students, for seven whole days. We discussed economic, political, and social conditions. We criticised authority and its trappings, along with repression, America, and Israel. We raised our hand to vote for or against, or to call, 'Point of

72

order.' We agreed and disagreed, we helped with the drafting of statements, shared in discourse and sandwiches, in anger, anxiety, and the glory of our affiliation with a student body with a high committee of its own choosing, whose communiqués bore the legend, 'Democracy all for the people, and self-sacrifice all for the nation'. We sent a delegation to the People's Assembly and the unions, and received a delegation from them; we got telegrams of affirmation and support, and we requested that the President of the Republic come and answer our questions.

I would spend the whole day in the hall, but as a concession to my father's insistent wishes I left the university at nine or ten o'clock in the evening. Shazli would escort me to the door, saying to me repeatedly, 'Your father is a reactionary, Nada. I don't see how he can forbid you to spend the night at the sit-in, and I don't see why you obey him!' Then we would bid each other good night. He would go back to the hall, while I turned toward the house. In this way, all week long, the discussions were repeated, until all of the participants in the sit-in were arrested at dawn, and my father sent me to my mother for fear that otherwise I would be arrested, too.

Was it a mistake to acquiesce in my father's decision? He couldn't stuff me into a suitcase, but he packed me off to France against my own wishes. He made the decision, but I accepted it. My self-doubt would trouble me for years. 'Fifteen hundred of your comrades are in prison – what are you doing here?' This question kept me awake nights, resounding in my brain until it became fixed there like information memorised in childhood. Feelings of guilt were etched deep in my consciousness, to be reinforced later by Shazli's words, half in jest, half serious: 'You went larking off to Paris for rest and relaxation, leaving the rest of us in our cells!' Contrary to my nature, I was tongue-tied, and shifty-eyed like a guilty child. I didn't recount to Shazli the details of the three weeks I spent with my mother in Paris. I only said, 'I learned to cook.' He raised his eyebrows in surprise, then burst out laughing.

Chapter nine

'We need you for an hour or two'

THERE WAS NO RELAXATION or peace of mind, despite my mother's solicitude and her wish to put me at ease. I had no access whatsoever to news of my comrades. It was not the era of satellite and the Internet. There was virtually no word about the students who'd been detained, no news. When I rang my father, he avoided any discussion of the topic, presumably out of a concern for security. Why did I go along with his decision?

In the morning, my mother would go to work, and I would take up a book. I would switch on the television, put a cassette in the tape-player. I would go out and stand on the balcony, return to my book, then leave it again to pace around the house. Back to the balcony. I would look at the clock, then look at it again. I didn't know anyone in the entire city. Gérard was studying at some university far away from Paris. I didn't know how to contact the girls and boys to whom he had introduced me; I couldn't even remember their names. The sky was always cloudy, and usually it rained. I would go down to the street, then go back up to the flat after five minutes. I waited. I waited until I heard the key turn in the lock, and then I would leap up to greet my mother with a hug, and after that we would fix dinner together, and sit down to eat it and talk. I would draw out the conversation, putting off going to bed, dreading the desolation that lay in wait for me the following morning.

On my first trip to Paris, Gérard and his engaging conversation had taken me from my mother, but Shazli, this time, had no chance of taking me far away from her; it's more likely, in fact, that he brought me closer to her, not because I wasn't thinking about him (I thought about him constantly, even as I slept under warm blankets, ate nourishing food, and enjoyed the feeling of hot water on my head and body in a warm bath, knowing all such amenities were out of the question for him now). My uneasy thoughts weighed heavily on me, so I ran to my mother – fleeing to her, as I see it now. I wanted to hear what she had to say, get to know her better, be closer to her, and I clung to her, seeking a safe haven.

'Mama, how did you meet Papa?'

'Mama, when did Papa tell you he loved you and wanted to marry you? What did he say?'

'Mama, was it hard for you to go and live in Cairo?'

'Mama, why did you and Papa separate? It's not possible that a room full of smoke or those hundred pounds he gave his cousin could be a reason to get divorced!'

'Mama, could we take a trip to Yvoire? I don't remember anything about my trip there with the two of you – was I two years old, or younger?'

'Mama, tell me about your father.'

'Mama, what was his relationship to my grandmother like? What did she do when he died?'

'Mama, do you still have family in the village?'

'Mama . . .'

She talked, and I listened to her, both drawn to and puzzled by the rhythm of her speech, the shade of her honey-coloured eyes. The sudden slight upward movements of her head that emphasised the meaning of her words reassured me and filled me with something as good as serenity.

The second week I decided to treat my mother to a hot meal she would find waiting for her when she got home from work. I referred to a cookbook I found in her library. The game delighted me, so I repeated it. Thus I discovered that the preparation of meals has its own requirements and rituals. I would select from the book the dish I meant to prepare, study the ingredients, and go out to a nearby shop to buy them. Then my mother called my attention to the big market. So I started taking the Metro and going there, not just to buy things, but also for the simple pleasure of going there: the other Paris, the one that escapes the post cards, the fashion shows, and the perfume advertisements. Women unconcerned about their full figures (unapologetically, insouciantly oversized), men in whom was combined the roughness of everyday life with smiles so sweet they took me by surprise with their, '*Bonjour, Mademoiselle!*' I would smile, make my purchases, and chat with vendors and with other customers. I would return home laden with vegetables, herbs, and two portions of meat or chicken, sometimes also flowers to surprise my mother the moment she opened the door and entered the flat.

This is when I started to develop cooking skills. I threw myself into it the way I did with anything new, but my absorption this time, in contrast to other obsessions, didn't fade away. It grew over the years into a serious hobby, one I both loved and was good at – I considered myself an authority on the subject. Every cloud has a silver lining: from despair combined with feelings of disconnection, anxiety, and remorse a 'super chef' was born. (I smile as I write these words, but nevertheless the description is apt!)

The secondary, and more desirable, effect of this new hobby was that it eased relations between my father's wife and me. Since the subject is cooking, I should say that it 'oiled' the hinges of the door that was closed between us, so that it began to open without the squeak that sets the teeth on edge. The first Friday after I got back, I announced, 'I'll make lunch for you.' My father was surprised and so was Hamdiya (if only her family had chosen a different name for her, things would have been a little easier!); I think she regarded it as a well-intentioned move to help her – she thanked me profusely, and praised extravagantly the food I prepared. Then we began to compare notes and exchange advice. I taught her recipes I had pored over in books, and she taught me what she had learned from her mother and grandmother.

Boring courses, intense activism, arrests, a journey, a return, and then activism once more. The result: failing grades in eight out of ten subjects (the two subjects in which I passed my examinations were unrelated to the field in which I had chosen to specialise); the other result was less ruinous – or, let us say, more useful: my having taken refuge in cooking gave me a skill that, if worse came to worst, might qualify me for work as a cook, and in fact for better pay than that of an engineer just starting out on a career!

My father was angry about my failure and upbraided me severely. Hamdiya came to my defence: 'Let her alone, for heaven's sake – what a rough year she's had! Those arrests, the anxiety, the fear, a trip she hadn't expected or prepared for

78

– what is she, made of stone?' She patted me on the shoulder and said, 'God willing, you'll pass with distinction next year.'

But that 'next year' in which my father's wife looked forward to my distinguished performance came with its own surprises and distractions. I switched to the College of Humanities, and my studies in the French Department, in which I had enrolled, seemed easy, since I was fluent in French and loved literature, finishing in two or three nights reading assignments that it took some of my classmates weeks to understand. But I didn't pass with distinction – in fact, most of my subjects I barely passed at all; two of them I actually failed, and had to repeat them the following term.

It was a year replete with interesting developments, starting with the appearance of three students from the College of Medicine before the disciplinary board on charges of having written for the wall newspapers, of contacting other groups of students, and of causing unrest. Then fifty-two students were taken into custody. So we began concerted action in seeking an appeal and the students' release, as well as an assurance that further roundups wouldn't prevent us from continuing to voice our demands. We held meetings, issued statements, contacted the unions, and staged another sit-in at Cairo University's Central Celebration Hall. Classmates of ours from the College of Engineering and the College of Medicine at Ain Shams University held sit-ins as well. Then they moved the sit-in to the Za'faran Palace, the seat of Ain Shams University's administration. There was another roundup.

This time I didn't go to France.

The knock on the door at dawn.

My father woke me up. He whispered, 'Do you have any papers here?' I gave him the papers. He took them, folded them, leapt lightly and calmly on to a chair, and hid some of them in the wooden frame around the glass of the door to the balcony, while others he concealed in the window frame, in the slight crack into which the pane of glass was inserted. Then he whispered in my ear as he turned to open the door, 'Deny everything, even things you think don't matter, and refuse to talk unless a lawyer is present.'

He opened the door. Two men in civilian clothes entered (later it became clear that they were officers), followed by three soldiers or informants. Three men in police uniforms stayed by the door, holding rifles at the ready. They searched the house, but found nothing. One of the officers said, 'We'll take her for just an hour or two.'

My father went quickly into my bedroom and returned with a small suitcase into which he had put a few everyday items for me.

As I was getting ready to leave, I said, 'I won't need the case, since I won't be staying with them more than an hour or two.'

'Take the case!'

I didn't notice Hamdiya there until she placed her own coat around my shoulders, with a large woollen shawl over it. She said, 'Look after yourself.' Her face was red, and wet with tears.

My father escorted me to the door of the building, where two police cars were waiting. They put me into one of them.

I hadn't been afraid when they were coming into the house and searching it, nor did the appearance of the two armed security officers standing by the door of the flat frighten me, nor the three armed men I found unexpectedly at the bottom of the stairs near the entrance of the building. But when I was sitting between the two officers who had taken me in, watching the dark, deserted streets, I was engulfed all at once by a feeling that I was suffocating. I asked the one sitting to my right to open the car window. I didn't tell him that I needed air in order to breathe, but this was in fact the case, no exaggeration.

Chapter ten

The Panopticon

I T IS FITTING FOR me to open this chapter by explaining the title, which may seem cryptic and elusive, as well as hard to pronounce. *Pan/opticon* is Greek, actually a compound word the first of whose two components means 'all' or 'the whole of', while the second means 'vision' or 'observation'. The expression is a term used by the English thinker Jeremy Bentham, in a report on prison reform which he published at the end of the eighteenth century. Bentham suggested that prisons be constructed so as to allow segregation of the prisoners, and surveillance of all of them by one or several guards. It was an economic project that would ensure through architectural methods a reduction in the cost of consolidating power whose hold on a large number of individuals requires dealing with them collectively.

The proposed prison would have a circular building consisting of several levels. On each level would be a number of adjacent individual cells, and at its centre would be a guard tower assuring continuous surveillance of all the prisoners, for each cell would extend lengthwise to the innermost portion of the building, from the façade looking toward the core housing the tower, to the outside wall of the prison. Each cell would have two openings, the first an iron-barred aperture looking on to the tower, and the second a window in the opposite wall to allow light to penetrate the cell so that the prisoner would be visible throughout the day to the guard on duty in the tower. Bentham suggested that the windows of the tower, in contrast to the cell windows, be enclosed with wooden screens, enabling the guards to see without being seen. He likewise proposed a design that would lay out the tower rooms in something much like a small labyrinth, preventing the prisoners from knowing by either sight or sound the position of the guard or in which direction he was looking. Thus it was all the same whether the guard was present or absent, whether he was conducting surveillance or not, for the presence of the guard would be a reality that the prisoners would internalise – it would be foremost in their consciousness and govern their conduct over the course of each day.

Bentham was well aware of the psychological and economic value of his invention, which he described as 'a new mode of obtaining power of mind over mind, in a quantity hitherto without example'.

Bentham's idea was regarded as a clear model for reform and was implemented in the construction of prisons, hospitals, schools, and factories; I encountered it in the course of reading another book sent to me by my mother when I was in the fourth year at university – Michel Foucault's book *Discipline and Punish: The Birth of the Prison*.

From Bentham's 'Panopticon', Foucault borrowed a meta-phorical representation of the relationship between power and the citizens in modern society, and how power permeates their lives, to the point where it becomes a part of their very being, ruling them from within as well as from without.

Foucault begins his book with pictures of torture from a period prior to the eighteenth and nineteenth centuries: flaying, burning, severing of limbs – mortification of the flesh before and after execution, always in front of a crowd of spectators. Then he proceeds to the new reform that conferred absolute control upon those in power without its having to resort to exhibiting horrific scenes of torture, and thus without the need for punishment to be publicly witnessed. Foucault elaborates on his explanation of this political mechanism, advanced by power, in order to command the bodies of the people and thus bring them into compliance and submissiveness so as to make use of their energy: a political economy whose sphere of operations is the body of the citizen, its instrument a set of methods that have been studied, calculated, and well-organised – capable, without manifest violence or perceptible terrorism, of carrying out its mission with increased precision and reduced expense. For among the advantages of this technology was the difficulty of tracing it to any single aspect of power, or any precise apparatus or specific organisation within the overall matrix, for it would permeate the social texture, distributing itself throughout and penetrating so deeply into its soil that it would become one of society's ongoing systemic functions.

Because in Foucault's view modern society is a thing of shackling and punishment, the Panopticon is a metaphor for this society and its various agencies. Foucault says, 'Why should we be surprised that a prison resembles the factories, schools, military barracks, and hospitals – which all resemble prisons?'

I was drawn into the book, even though I didn't understand everything it had to say. In later years I would reread it more than once. Then I sought out Bentham's book, so as to acquaint myself with his project directly, and this, too, I would read and reread. Each time, I picked up on something I hadn't absorbed with previous readings, pausing at a paragraph in one book or the other, and lifting it out of its context as if it were a picture intended specially for me that I had clipped from a newspaper or magazine and saved along with my other personal pictures.

This is not the place to discuss Foucault's book or Bentham's, to reiterate what they said, or to try to draw a connection between them and my situation. What I wanted to point to is that the concept of the Panopticon opened a door for me, inviting me to contemplate – obsessively at times, at others less so – the relationship between us and power, the role of authority in either subjugating dissenters, or destroying them whether wholly or in part, and the possibilities for escape from its grip through some form of resistance.

Setting aside Foucault and Bentham for the moment, I focus my attention on the suicide of two of my comrades and the untimely deaths of dozens more. I mean death, literally, fate and divine decree, as when a person becomes ill, his condition worsens and deteriorates, and so he dies; or he's not ill, nor does he show any sign of infirmity, until suddenly, without warning, his heart stops and he dies without knowing what hit him. I mean also the other death, metaphorical death, in which the body and spirit dissolve. The common element between the two is its premature occurrence, before the time when it would be normal and expected, before the person reaches an advanced age – say, sixty or seventy or eighty years.

I'll jump now to the case file – I mean two national security cases: felony case number one, 1973, the high court for national security, District of Wayli 131; and felony case number 113 for the year 1973, national security, Giza. I say 'the file' for short, because the papers that were filed exceeded two thousand pages and comprised numerous dossiers, including charges filed by the secret service police, information obtained by the secret service on the detainees. There was a complete dossier on each girl or boy, starting with full name – consisting of several parts: personal name, surname, and sometimes two middle names that identified the individual's father and grandfather – place of residence, college, and class-year. This was followed by a catalogue of the individual's activities, a summary of his or her ideas, the wall-journals he or she had helped to edit, and sometimes a transcript of things he or she had said, whether at a conference, in a meeting, or in a private conversation. There was a file consisting of statements by witnesses for the prosecution (secret service officers, workers at the university, sometimes even professors and students), and still another file, a longer one, containing the interrogation of the suspects. Finally there would be the order to transfer the case to the high court for national security. In the first of these two cases the transfer order comprised a list of 56 suspects (students, male and female, from Cairo, Ain Shams and Alexandria Universities, as well as one male student from Al-Azhar and a male and a female student from the American University, in addition to a journalist, a poet, and two workers). The second case included 46 suspects (the accusation fundamentally revolved around the formation of a group of supporters of the Palestinian revolution. More than a third of the suspects were students from the College of Engineering at Cairo University).

There were other files, of course, for similar cases from years before and after (1972, 1975, 1977 and so on), but I'm confining myself to the files from 1973 for the simple and practical reason that I got a photocopy of them from one of my comrades; the other reason is practical as well, namely that what I read in these files is a part of my own firsthand experience: the name Nada Abdel Qadir appears on three pages of the information gathered on her by the secret service in the dossier for the first case, and then the name recurs once again in the suspects' statements, at the top of 25 pages recording statements she made thirty years ago in response to questions during the interrogations.

I leaf through the files, read parts of my comrades' testimonies, skipping over other parts. I go back to what I've read before, read the dossier on Siham's interrogation, and then read it yet a second time – or a third, or a seventh – the same week, or a month or a year later, or years later.

'She was arrested, on the basis of a tip from the secret service, on 3 January 1973, after she left the University Dormitories, Cairo University. She was interrogated by the office of public prosecution for national security through the public prosecutor, Mr. Suhaib Hafez, on Thursday at one-thirty in the secret service headquarters, and the interrogation lasted until eight o'clock in the evening. The interrogator asked her . . .'

Then, 'On the morning of Saturday 6 January 1973 the public prosecutor – the interrogator – returned to the secret service headquarters to continue the interrogation of the student Siham Saadeddin Sabri . . .'

And again, 'On Monday morning, 8 January 1973, at the secret service headquarters, Mr. Suhaib Hafez continued interrogating the student . . .'

The papers for the case consisted of dozens of pages documenting Siham's statements in a period of twenty hours spread over three days, on each of which she was transported in one of the secret service cars, from Qanatir Prison to the site of the interrogation at Lazoughli. She sat before the interrogator and talked, after which they would shackle her wrists once more, and she would leave the building and the car would bring her back to the prison. She went and returned, went and returned, went and returned.

'Yes,' she says, 'I took part in the resistance to oppression and to the role of the university administration and the student unions in terrorising the students rather than representing and protecting them.'

'Yes, I participated in the sit-in. I participated in the march. I participated in the conference. I participated in the activities of the supporters of the Palestinian revolution. I participated in the call for establishing committees for the defence of democracy.'

'Yes, in my articles I criticised the authorities for their repressive actions and unjust policy in addressing national concerns.'

She says, 'On 26 December 1972, while I was at the College of Engineering, some students from the Law School came and told me that the student union was holding a conference there, and that any student expressing a dissenting opinion was accused of communism, and was at risk of being attacked with knives. And in fact four students were wounded and taken to hospital. No one was interrogated about that.'

She says, 'On 27 December 1972 the student union and the organisation for Islamic youth in support of the government tore down the wall-journals in the Law School and threatened the students with knives. In response to this provocation the students gathered for a rally, and it was my responsibility to move the rally out of the College of Engineering quickly, to avoid a dangerous riot. I stood in front of the crowd of students and started shouting, "To the courtyard, to Gamal Abdel Nasser Hall!" As the group was leaving the College of Engineering, the group hostile to us was calling out slogans against us and breaking the wooden rods used for hanging the magazines in order to use them against us as clubs. I decided to stay at my college to confront them. They surrounded me and said, "Get out of here, you Communist! If you don't get out, we'll pick you up and carry you out and beat you up. We don't want you to open your mouth at this college, ever." I sat down on the ground and said, 'This is my college, and I'm not leaving it, and I *will* speak. You want to beat me up, carry on." '

The students had begun heading down the stairs, and they found a girl, by herself, sitting on the ground surrounded by youths threatening her with clubs; they found themselves in an embarrassing position, and began to disperse. No one was interrogated about that.

The prosecutor general's office made no investigation into the perpetration of various types of brutality, such as the beating of students with truncheons and chains, on the day of the 3 January demonstration.

No investigation was made into the matter of the knife one of them was carrying and using to threaten the students.

There was no investigation into the injuries suffered by dozens of students, who were carried by their classmates on to the main campus of the university. Some of them had head injuries, and some were bleeding; others were choking from the effects of the tear-gas bombs, and still others were unconscious.

The prosecutor's office made no investigation into what the security officers did when they smashed cars and shattered their windows with huge clubs, so that afterwards they could accuse the students of causing unrest.

There was no investigation of what one of the security men did when he dragged a handicapped student behind him, yanking him sharply along; the student, unable to keep up with his rapid pace, tripped, stumbled, and fell on the ground, while, from behind, soldiers beat and kicked him, shoving him and trying to force him to stand up and run – he would get up and make the attempt, but, hampered by his condition, would fall down again, and the kicking would resume.

The prosecutor general's office never made any investigation.

I read Siham's testimony as if I were back in the 1970s, following in her footsteps. Having heard her once I had wanted to hear more from her. There were only three years' difference in age between us. What? I said, 'So it's possible.' If I hurried, I thought, maybe in three years I could be like her. A flood-tide of feelings; images, scenes, sounds, questions, all rise to the surface. A lump in the throat wells up, then goes away: pride, self-assurance. I know what it means to be innocent; the thought brings a smile to my lips. I'm no longer the girl I once was, but a mother trying to protect her little girl from a devouring world. 'It did devour her,' I murmur. What's done is done. 'It devoured her,' I say again, 'many times.' A shudder overtakes me. My eye catches the words, 'the aforementioned', and I laugh. The phrase is conspicuously repeated in the procès-verbal, and in the reports of the secret service, as it is in the charges brought against Siham: a comment in a wall-journal, the composition of an article or communiqué, participation in a conference or a sit-in or a demonstration.

In imagination and in principle it seems that the references of the secret service and the public prosecutor to those quite ordinary student activities as suspicious behaviour – necessitating secret reports and denouncers and witnesses for the prosecution; the knock on the door at dawn, the police on duty all night; prisons with budgets, administrations, officers and guards; vast blue lorries transporting people from here to there and from there to here; prosecuting attorneys opening investigations and closing them, applying themselves minutely to their signatures, followed by the date (day-month-year), after long hours of interrogation – this is what is laughable. But I laugh only at the words, 'the aforementioned.' No sooner does my eye fall upon the words than I start laughing – laughter I am at pains to keep in check, but I quickly discover, as it escapes from me and rises to a raucous crescendo that I'm incapable of restraining it.

Siham is not the only 'aforementioned'. All of them are referred to as 'the aforementioned' – my close friends, all of whose height and girth I know well; I know the lineaments of their faces in joy, anger, despair; I know the nuances of each one's voice and intonation; I know their gait; I know whom they loved, went about with, married; I know when it all came down on their heads, with or without their children looking on. Likewise I know a thousand details of their lives, of episodes both meaningful (the great, the earthshaking) and meaningless, or seemingly so.

I go back to the files, and all those facts slip out from their hiding places in the memory, to reclaim their body, their presence, their role in the creation of what I find written in the dossiers. And every time the same question surfaces: Does death constitute a barrier or does it, on the contrary, draw aside a curtain? For example, I read the words of my comrade who committed suicide by throwing herself, in a highly dramatic scene, from a twelfth-storey balcony. I read about the suicide after the fact and I wonder: am I seeing it more clearly, or less? Does reading across the line between life and death, across more than thirty years, with all that happened in the course of those years, form a thick lens, like prescription glasses, that improves vision, or blinders that shield the eyes from the sun's glare? Or is the whole premise inadequate? Should we consider each case on its own merits?

Be that as it may, the fact remains that the files are much like a mirror, in which I stare at my own face, which is not mine alone, but is rather the face that belongs to us all together, as a collective of young men and women who took part in a dream, a movement, a pulse; in terror and confusion and disappointment – a face some strip bare and then call history; others feel in it the throb of life and the structure of the consciousness it created, so difficult to annul, however rigorous the attempt . . . a mirror, or a group picture taken of us one morning thirty years ago in a sunny square. I look more closely, and cry, 'This is me, and this . . . Good Lord, look how thin he was, and that one . . . as if it were someone else, and here's so-and-so, may she rest in peace, and there – my God, how she's changed. And that one . . . incredible, he was so handsome – he still is, so why does he look so grubby and dishevelled in the picture, like a student's dormitory room that for a month no one has lifted a finger to clean or tidy? And here's Siham . . .' I gaze at her image for a long time, and see us together in Qanatir Prison, reciting a French poem we'd both memorised in primary school:

Le petit cheval dans le mauvais temps, qu'il avait donc du
    courage!
C'était un petit cheval blanc
Il n'y avait jamais de beau temps dans ce pauvre paysage
Il n'y avait jamais de printemps, ni derrière ni devant.

We take turns reciting the lines of the poem. One of the women on our cellblock objects, 'We don't understand!' Siham translates: 'A little white horse.' 'A colt,' I put in. She says, 'A brave white colt, they're behind him and he's in front.' I say, 'All of them are behind, and he's in the vanguard.' Together we finish translating the poem, or interpreting the lines when they're too hard to translate.

Chapter eleven

Incongruities

N O ONE TORTURED US in prison. We were beaten, we
girls, one time: on the day we decided we would refuse
to go back to our cells, after a rally protesting the placement of
one of our mates with the criminal prisoners. They descended
on us with truncheons; some of us suffered bruises or minor
wounds. But the era of Abdel Latif Rushdie had passed, or so
it seemed to me – this was one of my many naïve notions.
(Here is where Foucault's argument concerning the transi-
tion from securing power by means of extreme torture to
control by means of the Panopticon represents a European
reality, applicable only in part to our own situation, in that
for us power is like a thrifty, scrimping housewife, who never
gets rid of anything, even if it's worn out – she keeps her
old, used-up things along with whatever new things she has
managed to procure, usually in the same drawer, or at best in
two adjoining drawers, opening sometimes one, sometimes
the other, according to circumstance and need.)

We were not tortured, because we were students, and the
authorities knew how little threat we represented, or because
the new president had risen to power only recently, holding
the card of democracy: a democracy with teeth, as he once

declared, or one whose teeth had been pulled – it hardly matters; what matters is that it was a democracy that permitted the arrest of thousands of students, and occasionally non-students, in the course of a single night, and either punished dissenters with modern batons, different from Abdel Latif Rushdie's, or brought them baskets full of carrots, and patted them sweetly on the head, so that they took one look and turned into tame rabbits. (And as long as we're back on the subject of Abdel Latif Rushdie, that 'Abul Fawares', the ultimate cavalier, we must mention – though it's a digression – that he was transferred to Upper Egypt, where he pursued some of his usual methods, ordering his men to beat the soles of a suspect's feet in front of a crowd of spectators. But the victim was a man of position and good family, and no sooner was the family informed than – before daybreak – they had bombarded the cavalier's house. The government couldn't lay hands on those who had perpetrated the killing of its personal cavalier, whom it had mounted upon its own horse. My paternal aunt recounted this incident to me, and then later I confirmed the accuracy of the details she had related, when a former detainee, one of my father's colleagues, offered them up in a book he wrote.)

Abdel Latif Rushdie did not break us – he was off the set. Nor did the milder versions, those who took his place in the seventies, break us. What, then, broke us? And how?

The question that preoccupies Arwa – between two suicide attempts (the one that failed, when she threw herself into the Nile but was rescued, and the second, when she jumped from the twelfth floor) – is a similar one she takes up in the context of what she calls the attempt to identify both our 'true image' and the reasons for the 'aborted dream'. She talks about the defiance of that group of boys and girls who set out on their noble mission one morning, answering 'history's summons', wishing to 'adjust the scales', raising the banner of the 'dream of collective liberation', convinced they were a collective who were partaking together of the grand march that 'traversed the ages', 'toward fraternity, equality, justice, and fulfilment'. What happened to them, then, that in the end they were merely a generation come 'before their time' (that's the title of her book), living lives of isolation, despair, impotence and flaccidity, or else of nihilism, stripped of all morality? What happened between that exuberant moment of setting off to realise the noble dream, and the final moment of abandoning the dream to a life of 'wholesale destruction', where they became 'like mummies that, suddenly exposed to the sun, crumbled into dust'?

Arwa talks about the moment that empowered the students to announce their defiance, seeing it as a tragic moment, in spite of everything, because the establishment – armed with 'a long history of autocracy and the prerogative of word, deed, and thought' – had been on the point of taking the populace altogether on a different path, reducing it to a state of murderous mayhem, with society following submissively, disempowered and helpless, for 'it had no foot free, with which to keep its balance'. During the collapse, the situation and its rules changed, and 'the struggle reached a new level too fierce to be led by students'.

I don't know how comprehensive this answer is, as for the most part I am afraid of broad generalisations – that is, of absolute judgements or conclusive answers in matters relating to the history of an epoch or the exertions of a generation. All I have to go by is what I saw with my own eyes: a wave that swelled and receded. And because we were young, we saw in the wave only what the young see. We started out laughing, roused by the unexpected sport. Then we held our breath and plunged into the depths; one moment the waters closed over us and the next we raised our heads and took a deep breath, confident, declaring that we were the most capable of winning the contest. Then we would swim on, laughing, jumping, diving, surfacing, playing in the water. As the sun tanned our skin, we found ourselves and each other that much more robust and beautiful.

Hazem is irritated by what I say, finds my words provoking; he remarks acidly, 'Fill in the picture, *Sitt* Nada: the young people on the beach at night, alone, naked, and frightened, the whirlpools that can drag you down to the bottom of the ocean, the sinking ships! I can't take your overwrought fantasies. It's not about a bunch of children, the ocean, people feeling sad. The reality is more complex and more cruel – besides, we were never that innocent. The difficulty and guile of the surrounding circumstances were more than we could handle, it's true, but we, despite all the good intentions and the splendour of our collective efforts, were corrupted by a thousand things: from the little shops that treated the street like a puppet show whose strings they could pull, to the deep-rooted ignorance and stupidity, the miscalculations, and the high-handedness of mini-generals.'

'You didn't like Arwa. It was your right not to like her. But try to read her book objectively!'

'The fact that I object to shameless reductivism doesn't mean I've lost my objectivity. I recognise that she hadn't entirely recovered from her health problems, but her posing as a theorist upsets me. There are some intelligent insights in the book, but taken as a whole it's poor from a theoretical standpoint, marred by its own facile approach: "The bourgeoisie is the problem, and the behaviour of the bourgeoisie is responsible for every false step, every perversion, every failure" – what could be more convenient than a rack to hang our mistakes on, so we can wash our hands of them, and be relieved?'

'God, that's unfair!'

'It's not unfair. Any reading of this reality – which is freighted with history going way back, and with endless contradictions – requires of us a greater effort. It's a responsibility, *Sitt* Nada, and if we're not equal to it then we'd better admit it!'

'Her book is rather like passing reflections, her personal papers.'

'And judgements, lots of judgements, false generalisations, provocative oversimplifications. I think the split she points to between the ideal in her mind and the reality she lived is nothing but an internal split between what she believed about herself and the reality she disowned, even though she herself was part of that reality. Wasn't Arwa one of the leaders of the movement? Wasn't she at the head of one of those little shops? Didn't you tell me that, in prison, they wanted to break Siham because she wasn't one of their number? Wasn't their jealousy of her and her astonishing popularity a part of their motive?'

'You're harsh, Hazem, you never forget a grievance.'

'Maybe so. But I hate nihilism, and I hate seeing the people brought to despair by the fall of one person who, in his own personal state of despair, proclaims with casual ease that any undertaking people may turn to in order to create meaning in their lives is just tilting at windmills. In her book, Arwa writes that family, children, the struggle, are all imaginary solutions. By what right . . .'

I interrupted him. 'You're like some fool of a teacher with a metal ruler in his hand that he's using to beat the palms of a little girl, unable to see her terror and confusion, or even to notice that she's bleeding. Actually, your behaviour is even worse than that, because the girl you're beating died! How did you get to be so cruel?'

He got angry, and we parted.

Not all was well in my relationship with Arwa. Was it the chemistry that attracts and repels, or a difference in temperament and ways of looking at things? Or was it that the coolness that arose between us when I refused to join her group became like a snowball that just keeps getting bigger with or without cause? But at this point I wasn't nitpicking, so why was Hazem? He wasn't cruel by nature. He had been closer to Arwa, coming more into direct contact with her, for the collective embraced them both. Then Hazem left, declaring that the way things were being managed was ineffective, and would lead no one to safe ground. They didn't accept this statement coming from him; when Arwa herself, fifteen years later, said some of the same things he had said, and called her book *Before Their Time*, she found an audience that would celebrate her wisdom and cheer her on. Against Hazem, on the other hand, they had levelled the popular indictment: 'Bourgeois', they called him, saying, 'He sold out for the sake of his own personal aspirations.' In spite of this he didn't cut himself off from them – he would still be there to lend his support to any of them in their hour of need, ready to provide medical treatment if someone was ill, and quick to assist with funeral arrangements in the event of a death. He took part in

Arwa's funeral, although he had announced, when the news was first brought to him, that he wouldn't march in the procession. 'Arwa,' he said, 'spat in all our faces. I can forgive her for everything,' he said, 'except killing herself. That I can never forgive.' And yet he did march in the funeral procession. He helped carry the coffin. He accompanied the mourners to the gravesite. He evinced a strange grief I had never seen in him before – for grief is a powerful downward force, lowering the head and shoulders, as if the body, in sorrow, grew feeble and insubstantial, lending gravity the virulence to overpower it. But Hazem's grief was expressed as a peculiar kind of anger, rather like the force of a violent storm. It was as if Arwa, before his eyes, had split in two: a dead person whose loss he grieved, and a killer against whom he blazed with wrath, confronting her with a violence he could scarcely contain.

'There's more to it,' I thought, 'than just abusing someone he doesn't want to forget.' I rang him the following day, and we made up.

It's strange that I should cling to the same perception of someone for thirty years; that time should pass, years go by, the scene keep changing, and my image of that person remain just as it was when it fixed itself in my mind at the time of our first encounters. It is as if, by intuition or perspicacity, I had acquired, once and for all, the ability of that tall, slender boy to remain upright in a frightening scene, buffeted by bilious and pestilential winds. (Was it actually on a brilliant, sunny morning that we had that picture taken, or was it cloudy and ominous?)

Hazem grew up and so did I. We went our different ways, meeting on occasion by chance, or by arrangements we made through telephone calls from one country to another. For years we wouldn't meet, and then we would resume seeing each other once more, each of us finding the other just as when we last parted company, apart from a little weight gained or lost, hair greying or black threaded with white, a bout with depression just surmounted or about to begin – each of us found the other still alone, still a comrade.

I never fully acknowledged to him the place he occupied in my soul. I was in the habit of dissimulating, and of putting on the affability of a colleague, of joking and bickering. We would get together and laugh raucously. We would playfully trade off the costumes of a masquerade, and for moments in which confusion reigned be unable to distinguish between what was real and what was the disguise. We would banter and joke, and laugh still more loudly, like a pair of lunatics, mocking the world, playing with words. Or he might be absent-minded, impervious to humour, and then I might put up with him or not: we might have a row, quarrelling in loud voices, then abruptly going our separate ways, one of us walking away from the other in the middle of a sentence, in the middle of the road, giving both ourselves and the other a break.

Months would go by, and then we would start meeting again.

At some conference where I was working as a simultaneous interpreter, someone said to me – someone of whom I remember nothing except how blue his eyes were and how sleek his blond hair was, gathered in what looked like a short ponytail – 'To confront the system on your own is simply impossible!' I don't remember whether this was the sequel to something he'd already said and he went on at great length, or whether his commentary was confined to this single utterance. Nor do I remember the context. But this comment often surfaces in my mind, and with it a clip from an old black-and-white Italian film – by Vittorio De Sica, I think: a group of people, poor and homeless, who spend their nights wherever they find themselves. We see them on a very cold, cloudy morning, when they have just got up from their haphazard beds, clothed in rags that scarcely keep off the cold. There in the open they approach a small triangular patch of light formed by a ray of sun that breaks through the clouds. They stand together there, seeking warmth, pressing close and then still closer against one another, until none of them is outside the spot upon which the sunbeam falls.

Why did this clip, from a film I saw such a long time ago, stick in my mind? I recall the scene, then wonder all over again about the individual and the group. I think about the two-way street where the individual morphs into the group, or the group dissolves into individuals.

It dissolved, and yet my friendship with Hazem remained, warm and firmly rooted. Strange!

We met initially at the first big sit-in. He was sitting in the seat next to mine – tall, slim, and so young you were amazed he was a university student. I said, 'Nada Abdel Qadir, pre-qualifying in engineering, Cairo.'

'Hazem Kamel,' he said, 'medicine, Cairo.'

We shook hands.

'Are you pre-med?'

'I'm in the bachelor's programme!'

'Are you joking?'

'Of course I'm joking. I'm in my first year of high school, but I skipped school and came to the sit-in. I look a bit older than I am, don't I?'

'Which school?

'Al-Saïdiyya. Just a stone's throw away. I climb over the school fence, then it's a hop, skip, and a jump and I'm inside the university.'

When I met him for the second time I asked him, 'Did you skip school again?'

'They expelled me for skipping too many times.'

'What will you do now?'

'Look for a job – anything at all, because I'm looking after three children and their mother!'

For years these two encounters would fuel Hazem's mockery – he would ridicule my credulity, with a standard closing remark: 'Silly girl!'

After I got out of prison, I went back to my on-campus activism as a matter of course, although I was more careful about reconciling it with my academic requirements. More to the point, I was capable of reconciling the two, because I made up my mind to refuse to join any of the existing groups, those that demanded a great deal of effort from their young members ('the vigorous capacity for endless discussion that belonged to people with too much time on their hands . . . endless discussion instead of productive work' – in this Arwa was exactly right, although she herself had been among those with this kind of capability, and had been one of the pillars of these organisations). The issue of wasted energy wasn't the greatest deterrent for me – rather it was the contemptible situation I had experienced firsthand in prison, which all too often produced petty tyrants and a lot of iron boxes.

By this abstention I escaped the most confining of the Masonic circles – my relationship with, and estrangement from, Shazli was of a piece with this circumstance – and the movement seemed less forceful than it had been for the previous two years. Moreover, a number of its most prominent leaders were graduating and leaving to continue their studies abroad, going off to London or Paris or Moscow. (Sometimes it seemed as though things were turned around: the movement didn't collapse because they went away; rather they went away because the movement was fading, so there was nothing for it except for them to pursue their individual plans.) Siham and Tawfik separated. The breakup was cataclysmic, an act of treachery, out of nowhere. Stricken with a nervous collapse, Siham was beset and overcome by her fears. Afterward she told me, 'I lived in a weird state of terror such as I'd never known before. When a knock came on the door I was completely engulfed by fear and hid under the bed – as if hiding there would protect me from Them.'

I hated myself for opening the door to a conversation that induced her to say what she said. I closed it again hastily, and opened a different one. I reminded her of 'Spearhead', the plan we had agreed on the day we refused to go into our cells, after roll-call. (We stood in spearhead formation.) They attacked and we attacked, and after that we ran and spread ourselves out around the prison, so as to scatter the guards and wear them down. As usual, Siham was in the vanguard.

I said to her, laughing, 'You didn't have the opportunity I had, to follow the chain of events: You had a guard on your right and another on your left, and guards all over the place backing them up, all of them upon you. You pulled one guard's hair and grabbed the other one, giving them all a good drubbing with your feet. You were too much for them!'

She smiled. 'I was fixated on repaying them blow for blow. I wasn't thinking of anything except that I had to get the better of them.'

'For my part, I was rapt before the spectacle, and forgot to strike out, forgot to kick, forgot to be afraid – I stood transfixed by what I saw, rooted to the spot and musing on your ability to face down three guards all at once.'

We recalled the details of that episode and laughed over our failed battle plan, which ended with some of us beaten up, with those in front of the cells (which they had refused to enter at the staging of the protest) now wanting to take cover in them, while one solitary comrade actually accomplished the second part of our strategy – the plan to spread out into different parts of the prison: she 'scattered' all by herself, and so they ganged up on her and beat her to within an inch of her life.

I deliberately invoke the funny incidents, and we both laugh. But when I leave her and go home and get into bed, what she said about her fear, and how she hid under the bed, comes back to me, and I weep until my pillow is wet. I get up and spread a towel over it, but then the towel gets soaked as well, and I replace it with another.

I never told this story about the bed. Once, when I was on the point of confiding it to Hazem some years later, the words froze on my tongue, and I found myself saying to him, 'Don't you think we should establish a political association for orphans like us?'

He raised his eyebrows quizzically. I didn't explain. 'Just a thought,' I said. And we took leave of each other.

At the beginning of the following academic year, I took to reading whatever books appealed to me – textbooks or otherwise – without feeling guilty, or worrying that I was doing this at the expense of the cause. I began to express feelings of scorn and contempt for X and Y if I thought that they were stupid or corrupt; now that I wasn't affiliated with the organisation and its hierarchical structure, I felt no obligation to respect them and follow their brilliant instructions. The reaction of my comrades, who still abided by what I now rejected, availed nothing except to increase my alienation and my determination to accept what I liked and refuse what I didn't, following only my own head, even if some regarded this individualism as a residue of the 'corrupt petty bourgeoisie' to which I belonged. None of my comrades said this to me directly, except for Shazli, who flung it in my face one day – so we quarrelled bitterly. The rift between us lasted several weeks, and then when we made up he took me by surprise:

'Nada, what do you say we get married?'

'How can we get married and set up house when we're students? My father is paying my expenses, and your family's paying yours.'

'We can work while going to school.'

I laughed. 'How? We can't find enough time for studying to begin with – we don't go to most of the lectures as it is! Besides, we're not even twenty! Siham and Tawfik split up, Arwa and Khaled as well. It seems to me marriage is a strategic decision, to be taken by a person who's mature and self-assured. I laughed again. It's like those well-made commodities you expect to last a lifetime. I'm going to graduate from the university first and work for a few years before I think about marriage!'

He turned pale, then burst out shrilly, strident in his accusation: 'You don't love me. You don't know the meaning of love. You're just one of the bourgeois, and you think only of marriage bourgeois-style. Your revolutionary ideas are nothing but a superficial shell. You went to Paris for the pleasure and the spectacle, you threw me on the mat and left. Your father took part in the dissolution of the Party!'

He turned his back on me and befriended another girl.

Then began a new phase in my life, my responsibility for which I could not neglect, nor could I deny the joy it brought me.

Hamdiya took me aside, looking conspicuously pale and wan. 'There's something I want to talk to you about,' she said. I looked at her. She said she was pregnant. I didn't know what I was expected to say, nor did I know how to deal with the news. I said nothing, as if I hadn't heard, or had heard her but not grasped the words.

'I'm afraid to tell your father,' she said.

'Why? He'll be overjoyed.'

'No, he won't. He made an agreement with me before we got married that we wouldn't have children. I didn't intentionally break my promise – I got pregnant by accident.'

'Do you want to terminate the pregnancy?'

When she didn't reply, I said, 'Tell him in my presence, and then leave it to me.'

I surprised myself in saying this, not knowing why I said it or why I had decided so quickly and resolutely that I would protect her from my father.

After dinner, Hamdiya made tea and brought it to us in the sitting room. Then she sat down beside me and said in a faint voice, looking at my father, 'Doctor (for this is what she called him), yesterday the physician confirmed that I'm pregnant.'

There was a moment's silence, which was broken by my father's voice. 'It's not a problem. You can have an abortion.'

I joined the conversation. 'Why an abortion? Does she have some health problem that prohibits her from carrying and bearing a child?'

Neither of them said anything. Then my father looked at me. 'I'm about to turn fifty, Nada!'

'And your point is?'

I was gathering my forces, and it showed in my voice, which seemed louder than I wanted it to be.

'My point is that I may not live long enough to raise this child!'

I said, 'God give you strength and good health – may you live a hundred years. Congratulations, Hamdiya!'

Hamdiya was watching my father, waiting for a decision or a pronouncement, which struck me as provocative and offensive. Looking at my father, I said, 'Congratulations, Abu Nada!'

He raised his voice. 'I have a daughter, and that's enough.'

I shouted, 'But Hamdiya has a right to bear a child. And you have no right to deprive her of that, or to deprive me of a sister or brother. Hamdiya may accept your insistence on an abortion, and she may forgive you, but I won't accept or forgive!'

I went into my room and slammed the door.

The battle over the baby lasted seven days, culminating in my father's capitulation. Nor was this favourable outcome a matter only of the battle to save the child; it was also an occasion for collaboration between Hamdiya and me, as if my defence of her right to this baby conferred on me also some right where it was concerned – not merely that of the sister who would delight in the baby after it was born, but the right to participate in actual maternity, by following its progress from the early stages of pregnancy to preparing to receive the newborn, whose name my father and Hamdiya had given me the honour of choosing.

Chapter twelve

Lady Fortuna comes on the scene

L IFE CAN BE MELODRAMATIC – it can lead you unexpectedly to a series of events so fascinating and so extrava-
gant in their sentimentality that they lend legitimacy to the
Arab films we were raised on. For example, there's the one
with the child actress Fayrouz, at the end of which she cries
out in the courtroom, 'Papa, Papa – that's my Papa!' and he
embraces her – her adoptive father, the goodhearted vaga-
bond (Anwar Wagdi), and the audience's tears flow at the
happy ending. Or any number of films in which we follow
the trials and tribulations of the innocent heroine (played by
Shadia or Faten Hamama), who is usually young and petite.
Her cheerfulness is fortified by the horror of the evils she
encounters, and the cruel adversity she endures throughout the film, until the truth comes out at the end, typically
with the dawn call to prayer resounding in the background.
And since we all, to one degree or another, grew up under
the canopy of the shade tree that is Egyptian cinema, we all
indisputably know the meaning of melodrama, although we
may be unable to define it as a technical term (that is, we
are in the position of the little girl in Dickens's *Hard Times*,
whom the headmaster asks in the classroom, 'Give me your

definition of a horse.' And the child – whose family works for the circus, living among horses and dealing with them daily at close range – is unable to give the headmaster the scientific definition he is after: 'A horse is a quadruped . . . etc.') Life, then, surprises us with its melodrama, just as Lady Fortuna surprises us – she whom the ancient Romans envisaged as a blindfolded woman holding a vast wheel from which were suspended human beings and their destinies. The good lady would turn the wheel suddenly, at random, and those at the top would wind up at the bottom, while those at the bottom would come to rest at the top.

One week before Hamdiya gave birth, my father died of a heart attack.

He died before he reached the age of fifty. He died suddenly, with no telltale illness or pain to suggest even a fleeting impression that he might die. The men carried the coffin, the deep hole in the earth waited, and the mourning-women of the village began their wailing, which rose and intensified as soon as we drew near to the outskirts of the village. In a spacious hall designated specially for the women, Hamdiya stretched out on the floor beside my grandmother, who kept asking her if she could manage this, for her belly was bulging with the nine months of her pregnancy, making it rather a problem for her to sit cross-legged on the ground. After two days, my aunt whispered in my ear, 'Hamdiya's belly is very large – I've never seen such a big belly. She may have twins.' Then, 'Her belly has dropped, God help us – she could go into labour at any moment.' But the baby didn't give occasion for any further consternation. He waited.

Six days later we returned home from Upper Egypt, and on the seventh day after my father's death Hamdiya gave birth to a boy. Twenty minutes later the nurse came out of the birthing room, laughing. 'And a boy!' I thought she was repeating the news, either in celebration or in the hope of some extra compensation. It was only after Hamdiya emerged from the birthing room that I realised the nurse had been conveying to me part two of the announcement: Hamdiya had given birth to two boys.

And so the ending was worthy of a melodrama.

I didn't need to wait until I married and had a child to learn that a newborn in the house creates a magnetic field of which he is the gravitational centre. We circled in an orbit with the turning of the hours of the day – how could it be otherwise, with two babies separated in age by only twenty minutes? They demanded attention, they demanded care, and they demanded the provision of a thousand things large and small, all at the same time. So we carried them, rocked them, dandled them, nursed them, changed them, and bathed them. We bought tins of baby formula; we boiled and sterilised; we soothed and gently patted little backs; we changed and washed nappies and hung them out to dry; we rushed a baby to the doctor, ran to the chemist, and called the doctor once more. 'He's constipated,' we said, or, 'He has diarrhoea,' or, 'He's colicky,' or, 'He's got a cough.' We monitored body temperatures rising and falling, the appearance of skin rashes, infections of the throat. We noted eye contact, hand movements, teething, babbling, and the first word. The infants' first step – or steps.

It was clear to Hamdiya and to me that I was a help to her in the care of the babies, and I believe now, even if it seemed at first a matter of simple necessity, that this woman I had once referred to as a 'bit-player' had spontaneously relinquished a portion of her maternity, yielding to me a place in which to partake of it with her, while I spontaneously accepted her gift without taking time to think about it: accepted it easily and joyfully, albeit without feeling any obligation to say 'thank you' to her.

My care-giving and daily intimacy with my infant brothers wasn't the only source of my powerful attachment to them; it was also my feeling of responsibility to Hamdiya, a feeling that increased by increments as time went on. A month after my father's death, we had to make arrangements for how we would live. My father's career had been intermittent; he was incarcerated for two years, from 1954 to 1956 in connection with the case of the Muslim Brotherhood (one of the surprises my father bequeathed to me – I hadn't known about that first internment, had no memory or awareness of it, and stranger still was this connection with the Muslim Brotherhood. It had been classified incorrectly in the record, I think – or perhaps it had been misfiled at some point?). Then he was locked up for the five years from 1959 to 1964. The extent of his working life was comparatively short, as well as sporadic. His pension was small, and insufficient for the household requirements.

Hamdiya said, 'I'll try to go back to work.'

'Did you use to work?'

'I did work. Before we got married your father persuaded me to quit.'

(Yet another of Abu Nada's surprises.)

'Why?'

'He said the wage was too small to justify my leaving the house every day – he said his salary was enough.'

I didn't comment on this. I said, 'Then what will you do about the boys?'

113

'I'll take them to my sister in the morning and pick them up on my way home in the afternoon, four days a week. Then maybe I can leave them with you on the day you don't have any lectures, and the day your first lecture isn't until afternoon.'

But Hamdiya had no luck returning to work. She was in the process of looking for a different job when I came home to her flying high with news she received, to my surprise, with tears.

'I got a job – as translator for a news agency, with excellent pay. They offered me . . .'

'And the university?'

'I'll sort it out. I'll organise my time.'

She cried for a long time. I didn't understand what had brought on her tears. I was overjoyed at having found a job. Until the boys started primary school, I was the family's sole breadwinner, and even after Hamdiya went out to work, my material responsibility for my brothers was a foregone conclusion. I thought about their needs, and made them the highest priority of all I wished to obtain. I was concerned about the school in which they were enrolled, the book I wanted to buy for them, and the sport they liked, which I wanted them to have the opportunity to pursue. A second little mother – energetic, easily and naturally capable of accomplishing what she put her mind to.

Despite my new duties, I got better results in my studies than I had achieved in previous years, which had amounted to: total failure, across the board, in pre-qualification for engineering; in first-year French two failed exams that had to be made up (the year in which I went to prison, which was also the year of the roller-coaster with Shazli, by which I mean the rapid and vertiginous ups and downs in our relationship); 'satisfactory' in second-year French (the year my father died). Then I received a grade of 'good' in two subjects my third year (the year I began working as a translator), and I maintained the same standard the following year (the year I graduated and earned the certificate). I was advancing quickly and conspicuously at my job. After all, both the languages I was dealing with were my mother tongue, besides which it became apparent that I had a facility for languages; my Arabic was better than that of my colleagues who had studied at Arabic schools. As for English, which I had studied as a second language at school, I had mastered it well enough to qualify me as a translator in three languages.

The new arrangement, then, was evidently favourable, although I recognise now that among its drawbacks (perhaps the only negative result) was that I was cut off from the interactions of daily life at the university.

Shazli mocked me when I ran into him once by chance. 'Where have you been, Nada? Don't tell me they locked you up for a couple of months, and you got scared and said you'd learnt your lesson?'

The support Hazem gave me was limitless. I wonder again whether people have a chemistry that attracts them to each other or repels them, or whether luck, pure and simple, ordained that we should become friends and that our friendship should escape the cataclysms that so often strike friends and leave them with nothing but bitterness and ruin. Sometimes I think that perhaps each of us sought in the other a true sibling (it is odd that, in our relationship, the man-woman issue never came up), that maybe Hazem automatically, straightforwardly – because I was five years younger than he was – assigned to me the role of a little sister, and I simply stepped into that sacrosanct women's space. Perhaps I was in need of an older brother to turn to. I know, even if I never told him so, that I received from him a lesson that had a defining influence on my life: he had told me about his family circumstances, about his responsibilities after the death of his father in caring for his mother and his siblings – three boys, all younger than he. I saw with my own eyes, without his having said anything about it, the extent to which this obligation dominated his life. It had become second nature to him, a priority dictating what was possible and what was out of the question in every particular of his life. Sometimes I think that we grasped instinctively the value of our conjunction, so much greater than it would have been if we had subjected it to the violent tempests of fleeting relationships. (Daily, daily our classmates were falling in love, and whether it was for weeks, months, a year, or even two years that they soared aloft, it was only to come crashing down all at once. The boys as a rule were like cats that always land on their feet, or so it seemed to me: they slipped and tumbled, quickly and easily, only to climb up once more – these were nothing more than pleasurable adventures, no more significant than the thrill of leaping lightly from one balcony to another. The girls, while they didn't break their necks the first time they fell, bore obvious wounds and scars when they got up again, or such marks would appear later, after subsequent falls.

Perhaps I avoid discussing in detail my relationship with Shazli, because when we split up I didn't get any of those bruises that turn parts of the body blue, ache for a few weeks, and then heal. Maybe it would be overstating the case to say that my neck was broken or that I was hit so hard all four of my limbs had to be set in plaster. I'm exaggerating a little bit – but not much. Then, too, a fall from a high balcony happens once, and whatever will be will be. The relationship with Shazli ruined my twenties. For a year we were flying, after which for two years I was like a ringdove without a kindly rat to chew the net for me, and this was followed by years of confusion and bitterness, as well as withdrawal, in fear of falling once more.

Shazli confounded me with his behaviour, his demands, and his judgements – always final judgements that assumed his absolute possession of accuracy and truth.

In the beginning – blind love. Then confusion. The fact that I was young, inexperienced, and lacking in self-confidence prolonged the stages and made it difficult to move on. And the next stage was nothing but a kind of obligatory love, whose blind half deceived the sighted half, casting doubt upon what it saw.

Shazli had his seasonal themes, attached to each of which was a certain leitmotif he would keep repeating like a drone, although what they all had in common was that a particular purpose was assigned to each harangue. My trip to Paris had its turn; this was followed by the subject of the older Communists who had dissolved the party and sold out (in this scenario my father appeared as their sole legitimate representative, so it follows that the intent of this attack, inasmuch as I was my father's daughter, was that I should not escape the guilt my father had incurred); in a third season, my disagreement with his political analysis proved to him that I hadn't broken free of my petty bourgeois origins and the political alignments they implied; in a fourth, Hazem became the subject of the attack: Hazem aspired to be a successful physician, and selfishly made his work and his studies a priority – not to mention his pathological attachment to his family!

Seasons and stages, each with its target set up for shooting; at the end of a season, the target was removed and replaced by another.

I complained of him to Hazem. He said, with a dismissive gesture, 'Shazli's a twit. He thinks only of himself. He's a foolish boy, limited – it doesn't bode well. He may not even be capable of love at all!'

And because love is blind, I didn't believe him. I told myself, 'This is what he says today, so that tomorrow he can say, "I love you," and risk his chances on my answering him in kind.'

I didn't know Hazem well enough yet.

Chapter thirteen

A discourse on the importance of agriculture

I OFTEN WONDER WHETHER IT is intuition, that ability to sense things from afar, rather like the dog's sense of smell and its apprehension of imminent earthquakes or cyclones that causes it to begin to whine before people feel the earth tremble beneath their feet, or see the dark cloud descending all at once just before the storm hits. I wonder whether intuition is merely an automatic presentiment of a thing the mind registers before it is fully aware, or even recognises the perception. I wonder whether it was by instinct that I saw, before I was aware, that the coming years were to be violent ones, and more oppressive than any one person, or even a group of people, could face.

Sometimes I think, 'Nada, you're conceited and full of yourself. You're not so clever as to be able to read the future; on the contrary – quite simply, your mothering of the two little ones seduced you, it obsessed you, so you pursued the task passionately and to the very end: just another one of your manias.' I say, 'That's not true. The truth is that you knew instinctively that the humble profession of a gardener would be more useful in a drought. Which of the two is better: to die of grief, or to be absorbed in the cultivation of a seedling in a window-box, or of fava bean sprouts on moistened cotton in an old saucer placed at the edge of the kitchen window?'

My harsh mirror interrupts me, 'Were you thinking of how to be most helpful, or of how to escape and barricade yourself?'

My gentle mirror replies, 'Blessings upon anyone who is still of sound mind and spirit in a time of pestilential winds and the spread of plague.'

'Easy, take it easy. Let us review the cost once again – we'll go over it together, you and I, and neither of us will cheat the other.'

'I graduated from the university in the summer of 1976. I was able, after a year or two, to be satisfied with what I gave the boys. I provided the necessary financial support for them, leaving their mother to assume her own role in supplying their daily needs. I was still a loving sister and a young woman in her prime, living according to whatever the exigencies of life dictated and demanded. I chose the little ones, and immersed myself in them.'

'Why?'

'Because I knew instinctively that the coming years would overpower me, would overpower the efforts of all of us little clusters of confused dreamers, whatever our good intentions.'

'You raised the white flag, then?'

'I raised no flag, white or black. I observed, and my intuition turned to certainty.'

'Didn't that necessitate confrontation?'

I say to Hazem, 'You were born in the early fifties. I was born a few months before the outbreak of the Algerian revolution.'

'An overture like the opening chords of Beethoven's fifth symphony, astounding, catching you off-guard.'

He laughs. 'I refer, of course, not to the beginnings of the two momentous decades of the second half of the twentieth century, but to the appearance of my and your good selves upon the stage!'

'And the grand finale: the Americans' exit in full flight from Saigon, airlifted in helicopters from the roof of the embassy!'

(We hadn't arrived yet at the fleeing of the Israeli soldiers from Lebanon in May 2000, which I followed live via satellite television. Fretting over Hazem's absence, I began to whisper over and over, 'If only you had waited . . . why didn't you wait? If you had seen the hands beating on the gates of the camp prison, and then the gates opening and the jubilation.' He didn't wait.)

'Momentous decades indeed. An amazing time, between brackets – as if history had made an abrupt U-turn and decided to love us, accommodate us, treat us tenderly, and protect us.'

He interrupted me: 'By God, I don't know which is the son-of-a-bitch, us or history!'

'When it seems as though history's in our corner, we endure – or at least hope persists, even if we're weak.'

I go back to my two mirrors. 'I was struggling,' I say, 'to keep my balance and my self-respect as a productive and responsible woman. I watch the scene unfold, a poison dissolved in my tea and swallowed every morning and evening – no, not only in the newspaper or the broadcast news, but in the air I breathed when I went to work each day. For what's the shame in procuring an antidote like no other known antidote, sweet-tasting, a pleasure to the heart and to those looking on? Like the fava bean I mentioned, or a lentil, or a fenugreek seed on a piece of moistened cotton that I can nurture, and ease my mind by watching it put out its green shoot and grow a little bigger day by day. Call it wisdom or call it withdrawal – call it what you will, and let my mirrors reflect whatever they will reflect.'

Human beings are strange, seeing themselves as the centre of creation, of history, of the narrative. Suppose I had stayed – would I have fixed what had gone bad, would I have prevented the withering of the dream and the movement, could I, with two arms (not three), only two legs, only two eyes in a single head, and the only heart my mother gave me – could I have stopped the monstrous wheel attached to that dreadful harrow from approaching and wreaking its annihilating havoc in our lives?

My harsh mirror says, 'There were many of you – arms, legs, and minds; so then you redress the situation, and then there is honour in the attempt, and finally martyrdom is glory.'

My gentle mirror says, 'We did try, we earned the honour of the attempt. But in the end it was plain to see there was no point in foolish obduracy.'

A third mirror says, 'That's not a valid account. How can a person bear witness to his own times, his own actions? A dream rose up and was crushed. Leave the tale to those who will come after.'

I carry my mirrors around with me. They torment me. I spend a long time staring into them, then put them into a drawer and carry on attending to the requirements of daily life. Breadwinning. The education of the little ones. Companionship and the pleasure of watching them grow day after day.

Chapter fourteen

My aunt

I NEVER HAD THE CHANCE to get really close to my grand-mother. You could count on the fingers of one hand the number of days at a time that we ever spent together. I remember her at our home, when she visited us there in the company of my aunt early in 1959, when I was not yet five years old. And I remember her the day we went to the village in mourning for my grandfather (the day of the translation problem). I also remember when she came to our home bringing great baskets, hampers, and sacks laden with the delicacies she had prepared for us, to celebrate my father's return. Perhaps I met her on one or two other occasions, but I can't put my finger on where or when – whether at our home in Cairo or at hers in the village. I am unable to remember her appearance, except by looking at some pictures that were taken of us together. I stare at an image, trying to recall her face and its expressions. Her voice, though – the rhythm of her speech and her distinct-ive way of speaking – these I remember relatively well. She had a loud voice, and she enunciated her words clearly, her speech rich in imagery, as well as in its cadences and its diction. Her way of speaking had a kind of presence, whose differences and distinct qualities did not escape my notice when I was a child, even while it was beyond my capacity to grasp their significance fully, or to appreciate the sources of her expressiveness.

My grandmother died some months after the death of my father. I rang my aunt and let her know that I would not be able to travel and join her in the ritual observations, because the twins were down with fever, and because in just a matter of days I was to take my final examinations for the year. She heard me out, without comment. Years later, however, she chastised me roundly for my conduct. 'Auntie,' I told her, 'I loved and respected my grandmother very much – you know how much you all mean to me!' The truth is, I don't know whether what I said was sincere, or a mixture of sincerity and flattery, for I had surprised myself with my own words.

I rarely see my aunt, and we have spent only the odd week here and there under the same roof – which does not explain the closeness that draws us together, which is rather like a secret understanding, something that goes without saying. Maybe the reason for it is the strength of our mutual attachment to the same man, perhaps a shared, tacit admiration. We go for years without meeting; then we get together and the talk flows freely, as if we were picking up where we'd left off on a conversation already begun. I move familiarly around her house, sleep peacefully at night, and awake surrounded by a calm that amazes me. I contemplated this, wondering whether I was unwittingly replicating a romantic scene that had stolen into my consciousness from early nineteenth-century French novels and poems: the state of yearning to return to one's roots and antecedents, to escape from the city to the innocence of the countryside . . . and so forth and so on. I laughed at this notion, amused because I knew that there was nothing etherial or romantic about my aunt, who was realistic, practical, and earthly; to do justice to a description of her I would have to add all the synonyms the language has to offer. There was no place in my aunt's life for fragility. Ten times she had given birth, and of those she had borne five survived. She married young, and by the time my father had me, my aunt – two years his junior – had a daughter who was already married. (I no longer remember how many grandchildren and great-grandchildren my aunt had.) Her house was frequented by young and old alike, some who were connected to the household, guests who were as good as connected, others who really were just visitors, people in need of something or seekers of advice, those who came to assist 'al-Hagga' or who wanted to enjoy her company and exchange a few words with her. She, meanwhile, was like a bee, never stopping from dawn until dusk – working, issuing orders, arranging, directing, advising, remonstrating, scolding, rebuking, welcoming, and brandishing her sarcasm. (Did I get my own sarcastic tongue from her?)

Early on in my days as a student in the French Department I found myself laughing while leafing through books that contained pictures of Oriental women drawn by French nineteenth-century artists. Their imaginations running wild, all they could come up with was naked or near-naked women, and gauzy, diaphanous veils that covered without concealing anything of the Venus-like bodies. Black-eyed women of the East – and of the artists' fancy. My aunt's body was lush, tall, and full-figured, seeming all the more so because of the prominence of her breasts and buttocks, draped in her voluminous *jilbaab*. At night, she would seat herself on the ground with her legs extended before her, and I would sit close to her so we could chat. It bothered her that I wasn't married. She would declare she couldn't believe the young men were so blind that none of them had proposed to me. I would laugh and tell her some had proposed, but that I had turned them down. 'Bad move,' she would say. 'You raised your brothers, and now they've grown – what are you waiting for?' Then she would abruptly cover her mouth with her left hand as if concealing her laughter, or to prevent it escaping from her. 'Why don't you marry Salem?' I didn't know who Salem was, so I asked her, and she said, 'Salem is my daughter's boy!' She got carried away with enumerating his virtues, and I laughed.

'Auntie,' I said, 'Salem is six years younger than me.'

'But he's a doctor and he's very good,' she said. I can't think of anyone but you who would suit him. What do you say? Shall I fix it?'

'I'm six years older than he is!' I repeated.

'What's wrong with that?' she said. 'My grandfather, may he rest in peace, at the age of sixty married a virgin forty years his junior – younger than his youngest daughter. She gave him three sons and he lived past the age of ninety. Her whole life, his wife had nothing but good things to say about him. If you like Salem, take him!'

I hugged her and drew her off on another conversational tack, to get away from the subject of marriage. I asked her her views on life, anticipating the pronouncement with which she usually professed a reluctance that did not succeed in hiding her readiness for a conversation she actually found interesting: 'You ask strange questions, Niece!' She held back for a few moments, then replied, 'Life is both wide-open and narrow. When we spend it sowing and reaping, nurturing and raising, picking up and putting down, coming and going, going up and going down, loving and hating, enduring hardship and anticipating relief, it's wide-open. And as long as we're in the thick of it, with folks to the right and left of us, on top and underneath, everyone oppressed or overjoyed – everyone in it together – it stays wide-open. But if we stand back, we say it's as narrow as the eye of a needle, we say, "Why do we live, only to die? Why build when building ends in demolition? Why culti-vate what the wind will only take away? Why expand, only to open our hands and find them empty?" I say, when we're living life, we find it wide-open even if it's confining, and when we step back and look at it we find it narrow and suffocating, meaningless and pointless. For instance, when I buy chicks and look at them while they're little with their pretty yellow fluff, and I get to know them, and each chick is delightful, and I feed and water them, clean their pens, and keep company with them every day, watching them grow, my heart leaps. Look, Nada, if you think I buy chicks in order to butcher them after they grow up – me and everyone else – it doesn't change my pleasure in them or the fact that my heart leaps with tenderness toward them. Having children isn't like having chicks, and yet it is. I mean, I carry them for nine months, and my soul hangs on the baby, and our Lord takes him. If life didn't have its hold on me, I wouldn't conceive, bear, nurture, and rear another child after that. But life takes me and pulls me onward, and I go along with it. It gives, and I'm happy with what it gives; it bestows a second child on me, and a third; a fourth comes and goes, but the fifth stays. Wide and narrow, child of my brother.

'All my life, my body has given up before my brain. I go to bed because my legs are tired and my body is wrecked. In bed my mind keeps circling, it won't slow down or settle. When they took your father to prison, I kept thinking – all night long I would lie there thinking. Then I'd get up in the morning feeling suffocated, anxious and miserable. I had no desire to cook, or wash, or say, "Good morning." I asked him when he got out, "Did they beat you, dear heart?" He said, "They beat us, my sister, but we didn't give up. We learned, we built, we expanded, and we lived." Afterward I said to myself, "He was nearby, inside. I was outside, far away, standing on the shore and thinking, he's drowning, and my heart was distraught, but he was there in the sea, a drowning man, swimming." '

Suddenly she smiled. 'Did you know,' she asked me, 'that I wrote a letter to Abdel Nasser while your father was in prison?'

So my aunt, too, has surprises up her sleeve. 'Did you save a copy of the letter?' I said.

'I sent it.'

'Who wrote it for you?'

She laughed. 'That's a long story. I dictated it over and over again. Each time I asked the person who wrote the letter to read it back to me, and there'd be language from the newspapers and the radio. I don't work for radio or newspapers. They were writing things I hadn't said – one time it was "Immortal Leader", another time it was "Commander of the Millions", and a third time it was some big words I didn't understand the meaning of. I said, "Look, fellows, that's not what I said!" Then I called my youngest boy, who was in primary school, and I told him, "Copy what I say, and write it to the letter and the word – write it grammatically, and don't add or subtract anything.

' "Write, my son," I said to him.

' "President Abu Khaled, Gamal Abdel Nasser, Son of Beni Murr, and President of Egypt and Syria,

"I am sister to Dr Abdel Qadir Selim, who went first to the *kuttab*, then was educated at school, then went to university, then travelled abroad to France to work, in accordance with the word of the Blessed Prophet: 'Seek ye out knowledge, though it be in China.' When he brought back the required knowledge and began teaching at the university and doing his part for the good of the country, you put him in prison.

"We are honourable people, we don't call a dog 'master' and we don't bow our heads except to our Creator, nor do we ask for anything except what is right, and we ask that only of God and the righteous, for respectable persons ask nothing except from those who are also respectable. What I am asking is that the truth be established; I ask for an assurance of honesty from the officer who ordered the arrest of my brother, justice from the judge who ordered his imprisonment, and verification of the papers that were deemed a criminal act on his part, which merited putting him in prison.

"Abu Khaled, I approve you as arbiter, because I approve you as President of the country – how, then, should I not accept your judgement in the matter of my brother?

"The Prophet said, 'Each of you is a shepherd, and every shepherd is responsible for his flock.' I am helping you, Abu

Khaled, to carry the burden of an unjust judge or an imperious officer. Furthermore, I am helping you because in my brother and all the young men imprisoned with him rests the good of the country – how then can you lock them up and prohibit them from offering their knowledge, for whose sake they exerted themselves, and lived abroad? And how, when you yourself reap the benefits, can you prevent all the world from profiting as well?

"Finally, I inform you that I cannot read or write. I dictated this letter to my youngest son, who has taken the substance of my words and made it grammatical, without adding or subtracting anything. I have asked him to read back to me what he wrote, so I can be sure that he rendered my words accurately." '

'Did Abdel Nasser answer your letter, Aunt?'

'I got a letter from his office, saying they would look into the matter. I waited. After I'd waited a long time, I said to myself that either he'd received the letter and he was just busy, or else they'd hidden the letter and he'd never received it.' She laughed. 'It's a real friend who doesn't find fault. "He who loves you will swallow pebbles for you." Well, I worked out a pretext, because I wanted to forgive him.'

Perhaps my aunt enjoys talking with me because with my questions I give her the chance to talk about things no one around her allows her any opportunity to discuss. Sometimes she protests with a laugh, 'What is this, a television interview, my brother's daughter? You keep asking me, "What do you think of this, and what do you think of that?" But I have to say, you are clever and pleasant, not like the television interviewers, with their hair dyed blond and their eyelids painted purple, all dressed up like dolls at a fair, who talk as if they had a hard-boiled egg packed into their throats, and interrupt the person who's talking to them and read off a paper as if, heaven forbid, they were deaf and never heard a word he was saying!'

I laughed, and told her her opinion mattered, that it mattered a great deal to me. 'I want to know you, Aunt,' I said. She found this statement odd.

'What –' she said, '– you don't know me yet?'

Occasionally I am caught off-guard by the feeling that I didn't know my father well enough. All at once I wonder, 'What would my father have done in such and such a situation, and what would he have said about such and such an issue?' When this feeling gets hold of me I am perplexed. 'I don't know him,' I say, 'I didn't know him.' Then I fall to wondering once more, is it ever given to a son or daughter to know his or her parents well enough, or does knowledge remain ever incomplete and deficient? Perhaps that was why I kept going back to visit my aunt – the second reason, not the first, for the first reason was that I missed her and it put me at ease to see her. I would visit her and have long conversations with her, asking her a lot of questions and listening to what she had to say. Sometimes I would see my behaviour as comical and foolish, as I sat beside her in my trousers and shirt and trainers, asking for her opinions as if I were a foreign correspondent or a social scientist who had parachuted down into the village. It was she who dispelled this feeling by her spontaneous and sincere manner, which decisively established the closeness between us. She had never felt, as she herself told me one night, any estrangement from her brother: he had gone and come back, been educated, and taken up residence in Cairo, married the Frenchwoman, gone to prison and got out, and their relationship was warm, communication flowing without being impeded by any new developments. Perhaps her relationship with my father extended itself to me; maybe there were other reasons for this warmth, having to do with the chemistry that attracts and repels, without reference to any discernible logic; maybe its source was the wealth of affection that was apparent even in my calling her 'auntie', and her calling me 'my brother's daughter'. Each time I left, she bade me farewell with the same words: 'Don't be gone long, Nada,' by which she meant that I should not prolong my absence from her. I would go to visit her once or twice a year, and ring her up every week, to ask how she was getting along, and give her news of the twins and Hamdiya and myself.

On my first visit to her after Arwa killed herself, I told her the story. I expected her to open her comments by saying that suicide was a sin. I imagined the substance of her remarks: 'Our Lord alone reclaims his own – it's not right for any of us to take that upon himself.' But she didn't say this. She questioned me minutely about Arwa – was she married, and did she have children, siblings, a family? Then she fell silent. The following day, she brought the subject up again. 'And where,' she asked me, 'were you all, when she killed herself?' Her final comment: 'My brother's daughter, you either have to choose our way – marriage, children, kith and kin – or else you have to look after one another, each one being a mainstay to his friend. No one can live alone and unsheltered!' She said no more than this, nor did she refer to the topic again.

I told my aunt about Arwa (omitting some of the details), but I didn't tell her about Siham. Strange. A person talks about something painful in order to cover up the thing that hurts even more.

Chapter fifteen

Encounter

REAL OR IMAGINARY? DID I miss her so much that I heard her voice without hearing it, or was it she, herself, and I just didn't recognise her? How could I not recognise her? For weeks this question kept me awake at night. I would answer it with a decisive 'no', then contradict it just as decisively.

I didn't see her, for I was standing a few steps away, examining bolts of cloth, in search of something Hamdiya had asked for in order to make some duvet covers. I was inspecting the fabrics closely for weave and colour, comparing before purchasing. I heard her voice and turned quickly, calling, 'Siham!'

It wasn't Siham. I offered a smile that must have looked imbecilic, because the woman I saw before me wasn't smiling. She turned on her heel and walked off, heading for the shop door. For days afterward I was unable to overcome my conviction that the voice was her voice – for how could I mistake Siham's voice? But the woman I saw when I turned had been quite overweight and some years older, much resembling a housewife who spends her days at home, going out only when necessary, preparing meals and cleaning house during the day, and surrendering to the television at night, plying her knitting needles smoothly and mechanically as she watches, making a jumper for one of her children or grand-children. Definitely not Siham.

I kept recalling what I had seen of the woman's face – a broad forehead, made more so by her thinning hair; a double chin; dark lines and bags under the eyes, in a puffy, round white face. The passing face of a grandmother, who had gone out contrary to habit on a quick errand. But grandmothers, when they leave their confinement, tend to interact even with strangers, returning smile for smile, a conversational opening. This woman's face was stern, and she turned round abruptly, quickening her steps as if in a hurry to reach the door. Could it have been Siham? The whiteness of the complexion, the greenness of the eyes, and the light-chestnut hair were also Siham's.

I knew Siham when I was a new student at the College of Engineering, groping my way around the place. During the first days, the departments, the halls, the corridors, and the names of the professors were a labyrinth through which I made my way with no small sense of alienation and uneasi-ness. From a distance I observed the upperclassmen gathering in clusters here and there, joining together in conversation and laughter, or commenting on a wall-journal, or settling differences on a contentious point in the discussion. I noticed her before she noticed me: a large girl, tall and of generous proportions, distinguished by her green eyes and soft chestnut hair. I seemed to see her just about everywhere around the college, with various students, as if she knew everyone and everyone knew her. She would speak, and listen, become engrossed in the response to a wall-journal, or she would be contributing her own commentary to the journal, or just standing next to it, or leading a dialogue concerning what had appeared in it.

One day I caught sight of her in a circle of students, discussing something with them, with her eye on one of the wall-magazines. I wanted to join them, but I was too diffident, and remained standing not far off – or perhaps my feet moved without my realising it, and I drew nearer. She noticed, and greeted me, then extended her hand, and so I extended mine. We introduced ourselves to each other.

Then there was that conference in the Sawi Auditorium at the college.

The students filled the auditorium until it was packed to overflowing. Onstage was a minister who had come as a government representative, and next to him were two other people I no longer remember – maybe they were representatives of the college and the student union. Questions and comments followed rapidly one upon another, to the point of smothering the beleaguered minister. He seemed confused, either because the situation was new to him, or because he himself wasn't entirely convinced of the government's positions, which he had been delegated to defend. I no longer recall the minister's face, nor do I remember his responses, except one, which was evidently an evasion, and served only to entangle him further. He said, 'I shall refer your questions to his Excellency the President, and convey to you such answers as he chooses to make.'

No sooner were the words out of his mouth than Siham's voice burst forth like a missile, scoring a direct hit: 'If what you're telling us is that you're nothing more than a postman who carries letters to the President of the Republic, and brings back whatever replies he deigns to make, then we'd like you to inform him that the students will stay where they are, that they won't leave the university until he comes in person and answers their questions!'

The students were in an uproar, some laughing, some mocking and jeering, others agitated, infuriated by the minister's words. But some were silent, staring mesmerised at the girl, enthralled by the boldness and decisiveness of the words she'd spoken.

I was beset by doubt. The woman I'd seen wasn't Siham. She definitely wasn't Siham.

As soon as I arrived back home I threw myself into looking for the poem 'The Lament of the Little White Horse'. What I was looking for was not the original text in French, which I had memorised, but a translation of the poem that I'd done at least ten years earlier. I had written it on one of the pages of some notebook or other and then, in order to safeguard my translation, I had torn the page out of the notebook and put it away somewhere. But where? I spent an entire day searching – in the desk drawers, in my wardrobe, in cardboard cartons in which I had stored books and notebooks I didn't need, in my old suitcases – but I didn't come across it.

During the following weeks my fever of investigation extended to Siham. I went to her old flat in Giza, behind the southern wall of the zoo. I knocked on the door – knocked for a long time. She wasn't at home. I asked one of the neighbours, who said, 'She hasn't been here in ages.' I thought, 'Maybe she's at her mother's house,' and so I rang her mother and was told she wouldn't see anyone. I asked how she was, and was answered by the standard rote courtesy, 'Thanks be to God, she's fine.' I went back to her neighbourhood time and again; I took to loitering about the street in front of the building where her family lived. I thought, 'Perhaps we'll meet by chance, and then I'll know that the woman I met at the fabric shop wasn't Siham.'

Yet another of my sudden manias. I was possessed by the spirit of a detective in a mystery novel, or the investigator in a murder. I asked comrades and friends, when and where was the last time Siham had been seen. I gathered the threads and the bits of information. I compiled whatever I had, together with what I gleaned from others. I knew that, after graduation, she had worked – for some months, perhaps – at a private engineering firm, and that she had then left to get her doctorate in the Soviet Union, at the end of 1978. She had written me two letters from Moscow at the beginning of 1979, in which she talked about her circumstances in the city, her homesickness, how acutely she missed her mother, and the ferocious effects of the bitter cold. In a more lighthearted section of the letter, she told me she had gone to the Bolshoi Theatre, to the city's museum on a sightseeing tour, and that she had visited Chekov's house (she described to me his famous pair of spectacles, which she herself had been tempted to take off his desk), as well as Tolstoy's house ('I saw the desk,' she recounted, 'at which he wrote *Anna Karenina*'). She also told me about her rapid progress in learning the Russian language, and her classmates' astonishment on discovering that, in addition to Arabic, she spoke French, English, and German. In her second letter, some months later – by which time she had moved to another house specially designated for graduate students – she seemed less homesick, and she mentioned that her room-mate was from Aleppo. After that, there were no more letters from her, whether because of some omission on my part or because she was busy, I don't remember.

I was told by a fellow student who'd been in Moscow during the time she was studying there that in April 1979 they had staged a demonstration in front of the Egyptian embassy in Moscow, to protest Egypt's signing of the Egyptian-Israeli Treaty. He laughed. 'You know how big Siham was,' he said. 'We lifted her up on our shoulders and she began leading a chant, with us repeating after her.' I asked him whether she had begun to show any signs of illness at that time. He said, 'It may be that she had an emotional crisis – something to do with her attachment to a Syrian student, I think, but at any rate I'm not sure about this. Possibly she was disappointed in the system over there – the widespread bribery and corruption and other things she hadn't expected to find. Or it may be that she was shocked by the foolishness or perverseness of some of the Arab students.' But this friend of ours couldn't remember when Siham had left Moscow, or whether she had suffered from spells of severe depression during that time. Another friend, who was her classmate, said that her academic progress had been brilliant, but then she suddenly decided to terminate her studies and go back to Egypt.

Other friends told me that, after her return to Egypt, early in the 1980s (summer of 1981? Or 1982?), Siham settled in Cairo for a short time, perhaps three or four years, part of which she spent teaching at the lycée in Bab al-Louk. Then she left Cairo to live with her mother, who was working for UNESCO in Paris. At this point accounts vary, concurring on some points but differing on others. One person said she tried to commit suicide; said another, 'She tried to kill herself more than once, here and in Paris.' This one affirmed that she had frequented the hospital to be treated for depression. But one friend said, 'It wasn't depression – she was schizophrenic.'

This conversation angered another acquaintance, a woman whom Siham had trained and instructed when she was still a student in her first months at the university. She said, 'Who amongst us hasn't experienced depression? Who amongst us hasn't gone to a psychologist for help in enduring what we have to endure? She wasn't ill. When what was happening ceased to make her happy, she chose to find a way out. Wasn't it her right to find a way out?'

The episode of the zoo was recounted by a number of friends, although they didn't agree on the details, or as to when it took place or just who was an eye-witness and had been the first to tell of it. Siham had gone to the zoo, taking with her some colourful balloons. She stood at the entrance to the zoo, among the hawkers, and sold the balloons to children. (Some said that she was handing them out, not selling them, while others said that it wasn't balloons, but little toys she had made by hand.) A policeman had approached her, and she had to bribe him (the way vendors normally do) before he would allow her to occupy that spot. The vendors thought her an interloper who had imposed herself on them, to draw off their customers, which she had no right to do. So they picked a fight with her (some said they assaulted her physically and beat her). The story spread in the way that rumours do, passed around among the sons and daughters of the student movement, who were scattered throughout the country.

For several weeks I gave myself up to the investigation, but then some of life's other preoccupations distracted me – although not from the poem 'The Lament of the Little White Horse.' I decided to translate it again. I sat at my desk and rendered it in Arabic – a passable first draft. I went back to the draft and reworked it. When I proceeded to set down the final copy, I found myself substituting a mare for the male horse, both in the title and in the text:

The White Mare
By Paul Fort

Little mare in foul weather, what courage had she!
A little white mare, leading all in her wake.

No fine weather, ever, in that grim landscape,
No springtime, not ever, be it early or late.

Through drenching rain, she rejoiced in her freight
Of children, and still she led all in her wake.

Delighted, a cart drawn behind her small tail,
Onward she went leading all in her wake.

But serene as she was, so she died on the day
Lightning struck even as she led all in her wake.

Not for her then to see the sun through the clouds break,
For she died before spring could come, early or late.

Translated and adapted by
Nada Abdel Qadir

Chapter sixteen

Meditations on time

I WASN'T IN THE HABIT of keeping a journal, or setting down my thoughts or reminiscences, but one evening I wrote: 'Nadir and Nadeem went to the university today. University today, tomorrow a job, a wife. And I? Am I to settle for my professional work? Will I be free, ultimately, to carry out my prison-writings project? To marry? At my age?'

I was in an odd state – or should I say, a peculiar state, out of the ordinary, combining a profound sense of repose – rather like serenity, although it is difficult to describe it as such – and an obscure anxiousness, the nature of which I couldn't altogether pinpoint: as if, in the thought I had written down, there were some question my mind hadn't registered, dangling there somewhere, but eluding my grasp.

In the morning, while the boys showered and got ready to go out, I was conscious of a pressing urge to accompany them. I made the suggestion to them, whereupon they exchanged glances and burst out laughing all at once. It was an absurd idea, to be sure. I was sitting on one side of the breakfast table, Hamdiya on the other, in a corner of the kitchen. Hamdiya muttered a protective charm for them under her breath, stealing a sidelong glance in their direction, while I stared unabashedly right at them. Nadeem winked at his brother and said, 'Mind the cameras – they're pointed at us!'

Eighteen years – how did they slip by? In a flash, it seemed. I realised I was on the threshold of my forties: just two years to go. I hadn't noticed that the boys had swallowed up the years, the years required for them to grow from infants with their eyes shut tight, swaddled in white blankets, to two tall youths capable of opposing me in a verbal contest, and winning. The years passed smoothly from this point to that, while they grew up and so did I; and by a strange reckoning these years that were given over to the twins were not written off as a loss. They bestowed upon me countless extraordinary moments, whether of joy, confusion, anxiety, or trouble, but they constituted, at all events, a life. The white hairs that startled me in the mirror one morning were not invaders, but the natural result of a life I had lived. The twins swallowed up the years entirely, much as they might have tackled a delicious meal I had prepared for them. '*Bon appetit!*' said I.

No relationship or marital prospect I took up ever worked out. Because of the twins? There was love that took me by storm, like a lightning-bolt achieving its target. Then the only marriage proposal that appeared serious and promising ended in disaster when I said, 'Nadir and Nadeem are more than just brothers I'm devoted to – they are truly my children. It will be as if you were marrying a woman with two children from a previous marriage.' He was no fool – he said he knew this, that he had worked it out for himself, adding, 'But things won't always be this way. Parents become detached sooner or later; they'll be busy with a life away from you, and you'll make your own family, having children, and busying yourself with your own life away from them.' That was all he said.

I found such talk inauspicious – it seemed to bode ill for the future. I said to myself, 'If you marry him, some mishap will befall one of the boys, possibly costing him his life.' After thinking about it for two weeks, wearing myself out with the effort to persuade myself that my fears were nothing but superstition, that the man hadn't said anything to warrant such alarm on my part, I went to him, my mind made up. He didn't understand. I did no more than state my decision – I didn't explain. He tried to sway me, to persuade me – patiently, kindly, good-naturedly he tried. Then, the last time we met, he said I was mad, disturbed, unable to take responsibility. I left him, repeating to myself, 'There's nothing delusional about it – it's intuition, true intuition.'

My mother didn't like the twins. She thought they pulled me away from her. It annoyed me that she didn't mention them in her letters or ask about them when we spoke on the telephone. I repeated to her that for the first five years I couldn't afford a ticket to travel to Paris, and that the twins had nothing to do with that.

We kept in touch via letters and telephone calls, in general. I would ring her on her birthday and she would ring me on mine. I never told her that I resented her not having come to Cairo during the mourning period for my father. I reproached her, but without voicing my reproach to her. Six years after my father died, I was able to buy a discounted ticket to Paris. My situation at work didn't allow me to be away for more than a week. My mother was short-tempered and irritable. She said I talked too much about the boys. She kept forgetting their names, or getting them wrong; I would repeat each of the names to her slowly, but she would forget them or immediately say them wrong again.

Three years later, I had plenty of opportunities to do simultaneous translation, and this enabled me to travel again to Paris. I took Nadir and Nadeem with me. I thought, 'She'll get to know them and love them, and she'll realise that her family is bigger than she thought.'

I wrote to my mother, saying, 'This time I'll spend a whole month with you. We'll go together to visit your village, and you can acquaint me with all the places where you spent your childhood.' She greeted this proposal without enthusiasm.

I didn't bring the subject up again. I settled for confirming with her that she was to take her annual holiday from her job during the same period that we would be there.

As far as she knew I had dropped the idea of visiting the village. I hadn't, though.

It took months to get ready for the trip, since it wasn't a matter only of obtaining visas and buying airline tickets, but also of a kind of research and investigation – it made me feel like Christopher Columbus, about to set off on a journey to change history and geography, as well as the fates of millions of human beings. I would laugh at myself while I conducted my research by letter and fax, making telephone calls to put questions to friends and acquaintances and tourist agents. My mother's village was in Haute-Savoie, on the border of France and Switzerland, and before setting out I had to find out which would be the best, simplest, and most economical way to travel: to go by train from Paris to Douvaine, then by taxi to the village; or travel to Thonon – a neighbouring village, accessible by train, situated on Lac Léman – from which we could take a ferry to my mother's village; or to travel from Paris to Geneva, and from there cross the border back into France on our approach to the village. I needed maps, as well as information on distances and train routes – and the Internet era had not yet made its appearance, with the answers to all my questions to be found among its vast offerings or by sending a number of e-mail messages to people I might or might not know. I spent days and nights inquiring, gathering information, comparing, calculating, and, setting up budgets, and then replacing one budget with another. At last I made a decision – which, in its turn, required further arrangements: to register in a driving school and then apply for an Egyptian driving licence, which would in turn enable me to acquire an international driving licence.

Appropriate arrangements were made for my mother's sixtieth birthday. It was going to be a surprise, which would please her, just as visiting her village after so many years away from it would please her. She would see the house in which she had been born, the streets she had trodden in her girlhood, the lake she had swum in, the beach on which she had raced on her bicycle with a boy or girl her age. She would say, 'Here . . . in this spot . . . in this corner . . . on this hill . . . your grandfather was sitting here when . . . and your grandmother was standing there on the day that . . .' My imagination ran ahead of the visit, racing toward it, elated at the gift I was giving my mother, and longing for what I had not lived of my mother's childhood and her personal history.

It was a fiasco from the start.

My mother, when I revealed to her my planned itinerary, said, 'We can leave the twins in Paris – we'll only be gone five days!'

At that moment the child I had been reared her head. She was ready to scream at my mother that she was heartless and mad. I scolded the child, 'Shame on you, you little devil!' and answered my mother calmly, 'The twins are only nine years old and they don't speak French. What you're suggesting is impractical.'

She added insult to injury. 'You're doubling your expenses unnecessarily. It would have been better not to bring them with you to France, since you have this idea of going to Yvoire.'

I paid no attention to what she'd said. I began telling her all about the arrangements and the plan, but she wasn't listening.

Then the express train to Geneva: four hours. One night in a Geneva hotel. In the morning, a rental car, which I drove over the border to Yvoire. Two nights in a hotel and a day in Annecy. Back to Geneva, and another night in a hotel. In the morning, the train back to Paris.

My mother spoiled the trip. She spoiled it deliberately and systematically. She ruined every aspect of it, every single day of it, wilfully, as if she had made an earnest decision to do so, then put it into action, exerting her efforts to the utmost degree in order to carry out her purpose. I bear witness that she succeeded magnificently in this. When we got back to Paris, she and I quarrelled bitterly. She said that, for me, the trip to Yvoire had been merely a sightseeing tour. She said, 'You chose a tourist town that would amuse you and the twins to visit.' Her words were inordinately cruel. She added, 'I can't put up with the twins any longer – it's annoying to me, having them here!'

I took the twins and went to a hotel, and didn't see her again until a few hours before we left France, to say goodbye.

I travelled for the last time from Cairo to France in haste, because my mother was in the hospital. I attended her for a week. I kissed her forehead and her hands and went on kissing them. I kept saying, 'Don't be angry with me!' She smiled weakly and said, '*C'est la vie.*' Then she added, 'Life is strange!' The following three days I visited her in the intensive care unit. I wasn't allowed to go in. I would stand in the doorway, despite the amazement of the doctors and the hospital staff.

And then she died.

I spent a week in her flat, sleeping in her bed, bathing with her soap, drying myself with towels she had used, and eating from tins she had bought. For the first four days that was all I did. On the fifth day, although I hadn't set an alarm clock, I was roused from sleep as if an alarm had woken me. I said to myself, 'There are only two more days.' I began organising her things: her clothes, her underwear, her towels and bed linen. I folded everything and put it in a large cardboard box. I put shoes and handbags into another, smaller box. I put books into a third box. Then I transferred them one by one to a huge receptacle, in a nearby street, bearing the name of a charity organisation. On the way back home I bought a sandwich, a bottle of juice, and an orange. I put them in the kitchen and began on the papers and photographs: my mother's birth certificate and those of her parents; her marriage licence and divorce certificate, her identity card, her passport, her ATM card, and her health insurance card. I put all this into a folder and turned to the photographs: pictures of her, of us, of my father, and of her mother and father; pictures from Paris, from Yvoire – her birthplace – in Annecy, where she had taken trips with her classmates; pictures from Cairo and Alexandria and pictures from the village, with my grandmother and my aunt. I carefully wrapped the photographs in a handkerchief and consigned them to another folder. Then I turned to the letters: letters from her parents and from friends, papers in her handwriting and a medium-sized journal in which she had kept some notes – sporadic ones that she would begin writing and then stop. I placed the papers in a leather portfolio and put it with the two folders into the hand-luggage I had brought with me to carry on the aeroplane. To these things I added her two pairs of prescription glasses. In the bag with my clothing I put three of her dresses that I had always loved to see her wear, one of her bed sheets, a headscarf, and a shawl she had used during my previous visit to her. I added five of her books, and then packed my clothes. I ate the sandwich and the orange, and drank the juice. I sat in front of the television, where I drifted off to sleep lying fully-clothed on the sofa, and didn't awaken until morning.

I made myself a cup of coffee, which I drank with what was left of some pieces of toast that I found in the kitchen. Then I started on her bedroom. I swept the room, washed the window and its wooden shutters; I polished the bed-frame, the wardrobe, and the dressing table; and I sprayed the mirror with glass-cleaner and scoured it. Then I resumed my assault on the sitting room. After that I moved on to the bathroom. I washed down the walls, the bathtub, the sink, and a glass shelf on which partially used bottles of liquid soap and various creams rested; having finished with that, I scrubbed the floor. Then the kitchen: the refrigerator, the wooden cupboard, the round table, the two windows, the floor, and the walls.

When I was finished, I looked around at the flat. 'She'd be happy with these results,' I murmured. I considered going out to get dinner, then thought better of it. The idea of going out and walking to a restaurant seemed more uncomfortable than going hungry. I went into her bedroom, got into bed, and slept.

In the morning, I left the flat. I turned over the key to the doorman, made my way to the Metro station, and from there to the airport.

Hamdiya chided me for coming home in brown trousers and a yellow blouse. 'It won't do,' she said. She bought me some black clothes and insisted that we hold a night of mourning. She said, 'You announce it in the paper, receive whoever attends, and Nadir and Nadeem stand with you to receive condolences on the death of their grandmother. (I was startled that she should come to this simple and spontaneous conclusion that my mother was their grandmother.) She said, 'We'll distribute alms for her soul – did she convert to Islam?' I didn't reply, because I didn't know. My silence made Hamdiya uncomfortable. 'I'm asking you,' she explained, 'so that I'll know, if she did convert, to play a recording of the Qur'an during the mourning. I think it would be appropriate, even if she didn't convert – we should recite from the Qur'an for her and pray for mercy on her soul.'

That year I was stricken by the first of my bouts of depression.

Chapter seventeen

The unfinished letter

I DIDN'T NOTICE THE LETTER was there until after I got back to Cairo. I was sorting the papers and filing them in folders, so as to preserve them, and it caught my attention. How odd: a letter from my mother, addressed to me, that she had never sent, or even finished, although it was exceptionally long. The date at the top indicated that she had written it about two months after that catastrophic trip I had dreamed would make her happy, but which instead became an ordeal for me and for her. I wondered, why didn't she send it? Why didn't she finish it?

My mother wrote:

Dear Nada,

No doubt you remember that extraordinary night when Gamal Abdel Nasser resigned in a speech that was broadcast live on television. You remember how your father wept, certainly, but I don't know whether you remember what he said to me when I told him I didn't understand why he was crying over a man who had sentenced him to five years in prison. He shouted at me that I was blind, and he stormed out. You may not remember his saying these words, but he did. To me, those words were the final and irreversible separation between us. The differences between us, and our continual rows, were, for me at least, open to negotiation and reconsideration – differences that didn't mean the end of the world or of our relationship. But when he told me I was blind I knew immediately that our relationship was over, not because I was angry at some insult he'd flung in my face, but because I was convinced that I could never see what he saw: and I think when something like this happens it means that the break has come, and that any subsequent attempt to make it up will be merely redundant.

I left Cairo with so much heavy baggage, I don't know how I was able to carry it. I was going alone, leaving behind me my only daughter, the man I had loved and a relationship upon which my world was founded – I left all these behind me like a house destroyed by an earthquake. Then, too, there was one other bag I carried that was perhaps heavier than all the others. I was wondering: *Am* I blind? And if I am blind, then is this blindness an inherent defect over which I have no control, or is that I didn't know, or couldn't find a way, to look and to see? It may seem like a silly or trivial question, but it continued to dog me for months, perhaps years. I don't know Arabic. I lived for years in Egypt, and I was unable to speak the Arabic language, much less master it. I didn't understand your grandmother or your aunt, I didn't altogether understand the neighbours, and among Egyptian women I had no close friend. I was on amicable terms with many of them, but I lived in a state of peculiar disorientation, which no doubt I will describe to you in detail someday.

I'm a village girl, Nada, from a border town a long way from Paris. You know this. You also know that I come from a family of fishermen: my father and grandfathers were fishermen – which is to say, we were never wealthy, never noted for anything of consequence. (Perhaps it was a shared feeling of alienation that brought your father and me together – initially, I mean. My words may be imprecise; I was struck by the handsome figure he cut, and he said that he likewise found me pretty, but I feel sure that some sense of dislocation drew us to each other.) I fell in love with your father, and so we married and moved to Egypt.

Even now I don't completely understand how people saw me, or the ways in which they dealt with me. I found myself all at once in an unfamiliar situation. I wasn't Madeleine the village girl, a typist who lived in Paris among the marginalised; rather I was Madame Selim, the Frenchwoman, wife of the university professor – even if he was in prison – teacher of French at a school whose pupils were mostly daughters of the upper class. Suddenly I was possessed of a kind of authority – it was like a cloak that had been thrown over my body. I saw other Frenchwomen in Egypt, wearing the same cloak and proud of it as if it were an expensive fur coat. As far as I was concerned, the cloak was more like a coat of thorns – or let me call it, rather, a strange garment that made me uncomfortable because I didn't recognise myself in it. All that remained to me was my relationship with your father. And when he told me I was blind, there was nothing left to induce me to persevere. I left, only to discover afterward that a world, whether here or there, no longer existed for me. I discovered that, even after years of separation from the man I loved, his marriage to another woman angered me, and his having children with her angered me still more. There he was, falling in love, getting married, and having children, while at the same time he still stood as an obstacle between me and everyone else. I had no luck forming any comparable relationship with another man. He ruined my life, but here's the paradox: He ruined it after we separated, not before. This is a long story, at any rate, that I don't want to go into. I got caught up in my reminiscences, and have written things I didn't mean to write, entangled in my own words, on subjects I didn't and don't want to discuss.

Meaning to please me, you paid more than you could afford so that we might go to Yvoire. I should have told you candidly that I didn't want to go. Yes, I was frightened of that journey. But I also wanted it – otherwise, how do you explain my having gone along with your insistence and submitted to the temptation of returning to Yvoire, even though I was apprehensive about it?

My previous visit to the village had been painful beyond imagining. I hadn't yet recovered from that pain, or become reconciled to the reality that my village – that familiar realm minutely connected in a thousand ways to my childhood and youth – had metamorphosed into something resembling a railway station, or a marketplace well-trodden by the feet of people passing through, or a tourist resort accessible to anyone having the price of admission. The great big tourist buses were the first thing I saw when I came in sight of the village: a suitable prelude to what I would see moments later in the village itself. The place had changed, utterly changed. The narrow, cobble-stone streets remained the same as they'd always been; the houses still stood, as ever at close quarters; the old fortress; the church; the lake – all attesting that this was Yvoire and not some other village, but it had become a different village, taken over by hordes of tourists who filled the streets and alleyways with their languages and loud voices and the flashes of the cameras slung around their necks, until it was time for them to move on to the next village on their holiday itinerary. Chic restaurants and cafés for an affluent clientele. And to top it all off, I couldn't find the way to our house. How could that be? I passed the house twice without recognising it, and was disoriented for a moment, finding everything thrown into confusion. I went back to where the house should be. 'Here is our house,' I said. But where? Before me was one of those souvenir shops catering to the tourists. Then I caught sight of my mother: ample, smiling, doing a brisk trade with the tourists. I went in and hugged her, but we had no chance to exchange more than a few words, for the tourists were waiting, holding colourful postcards or clutching wooden dolls they wanted to buy, or looking to ask the price of some memento or other. I left her to carry on her business with the tourists, and went into the house to see my father. Where had the house gone? It had been eaten by a wolf. The façade of the house, two of its rooms, and the little garden, once my father's refuge after he retired from fish-ing, had been appropriated by the shop and its rose-bedecked entryway. The wolf had left only one gloomy room leading onto a small kitchen, and the toilet. 'How does Papa spend his days, Mama?' She said with a dismissive gesture, 'He's always complaining, but I'm busy with the shop.'

I foresaw that it would be painful to go back again, and yet I was unable to resist. I accepted your invitation, and so we went. It wasn't my intention to give voice to my distress or pass it along to you. I said to myself, 'Nada won't notice anything.' I made up my mind that my previous visit must have been tantamount to an immunisation, at least to some degree, and that this would enable me to contain my reactions. How did things get out of control? This whole letter, Nada, as I hope you have inferred, is an attempt to explain why the situation got away from me. No, it wasn't because my father, and then after him my mother, had died, but because this time I went back to the village bringing tourists with me. I'm not criticising you – I swear that I'm not criticising you. That beautiful village on the shores of Lac Léman – I was paying it a fleeting visit. I read in the tourist literature about a magnificent garden called 'The Garden of the Five Senses'. I said to myself, 'My daughter is blind.' Now, two months after the fact, I declare that anyone who is ignorant of a place is blind – no more, no less. And when I say 'ignorant of a place' I'm not talking about a road map or where the route begins and ends, but about a place that is specific to us, in which our own story resides, and which houses our five senses. I must admit, the presence of the twins exacerbated the difficulty. I couldn't endure their noise and their demands; I hadn't, in the first place, been able to accept that they were the children of another woman with whom my husband had been intimate.

In short, Nada, the trip was a disaster because I knew for certain then that my alienation was total, whether in

Yvoire, in Paris, or in Cairo. It was clear that, unwittingly – in a way it was sheer madness – I had made up my mind and decided to go with you to Yvoire, fortified by your presence, as if your being with me would dissipate some of the sense of alienation, and relieve me of it. But I saw my daughter as a tourist in my own birthplace, and I lost my reason.

I'll leave this letter now and finish it tomorrow, or the day after.

My mother didn't finish the letter the following day or on any subsequent day. She left it incomplete, and thus I would never have an opportunity to read it except after her death.

I folded the letter, and left the house.

Chapter eighteen

The twins

WHEN THE TWINS WERE small, Hamdiya tended to buy matching garments for them, but I pointed out to her that it would be better to buy them each different clothes. They became accustomed to this, and, as they grew older, each of them would choose according to his own taste and inclination. They looked similar, although they were not identical: brothers joined by blood and genetic background and by whatever stimuli they were both exposed to every day – the same kindergarten, school, classroom, teachers, classmates, friends, and daily routine. And because human beings are like mirrors, the features of one person reflected to a considerable degree in those of the next, Nadir and Nadeem looked more alike than they actually were. Nadir was not as tall as his brother, his complexion and his eyes were darker, and his hair was coarser. It was easy to tell that they were twins until they got to high school. Thereafter they differed more, for Nadir chose to grow a moustache and a close-trimmed beard, which covered his whole chin and made him look rather like a young French writer of the late nineteenth century. His brother's moustache, on the other hand, stayed downy until he went to university. When his facial hair began to grow thicker after that he would shave every day. Their voices were very similar, identical in timbre, so that neither Hamdiya nor I could distinguish between them at the start of a telephone conversation, or when one of them called from the bathroom to ask for a towel. Beyond that it was possible to tell the difference, because each had a particular rhythm to his speech.

It is my conviction that seeds sprout by their own inscrutable law, their own particular logic as regards both nature and nurture. From me the twins got their sense of irony and their scepticism, which I resolutely insist are characteristics of intelligence. Nadir, though – the elder by twenty minutes – was more bitingly ironic than the source of his instruction. Perhaps it was the era he grew up in that induced him to look at the world with a cynical and unforgiving eye. And yet his era was also his brother's – what about that? Nadir would startle me with his ideas:

'I'm going to study computer engineering. There's a demand for it in the labour market. If I do well, I can work for Microsoft, and go and live abroad.'

Troubled, I refrained from comment. I turned to Nadeem, who said, 'I'm going to study architecture.'

The boys graduated from high school. I had promised to take them to Paris if they did well. I didn't say that I would have taken them regardless of their performance, superior or not. I had a pressing desire to visit my mother's grave, and I didn't want to go alone.

Life is so strange, so bizarre – is it by strength or by selfishness that one prevails? As soon as we arrived in Paris we went together to visit the cemetery. I regretted bringing Nadir and Nadeem with me. I tried to hold myself back, but my resistance was in vain – I began to weep. I wept until Nadeem turned his face away to hide his own tears from me and from Nadir.

Nadir played the clown on our way back, telling comical anecdotes – the story of a fellow who said this, and a girl who did that, and a day when such-and-such happened, and another day when – scarcely stopping for breath as he leapt from one story to another, until he managed to get the result he was looking for: by the time we stopped for dinner before arriving back home, we were chatting as usual.

Before we left, I went back to visit my mother. I didn't cry. I engaged her in a long conversation – any passerby who saw me would have concluded that here was a woman who had lost her mind. I talked at length about her, myself, and my father. Also about Hamdiya and the boys. I said, 'You didn't accept them, but they are your grandsons – they know your name, what you look like, and the things you've said. They know about the fat woman you were talking with on the train, the quarrel that arose between you and my aunt and ended with a severing of relations. They know how you respond when you are possessed by anger, what you do when you give way to sweetness and your good nature wins out against whatever caused the tension. They came to visit you, just as they go every year to visit their father's grave in Upper Egypt, and one day they may come when I'm gone, and ease your loneliness by talking to you about me and about my father, gathering our three graves together into one, dispersed though they may be.'

I told her, 'I forgave you for moving to Paris. I didn't realise at first how angry and upset I was about that move. When

I did acknowledge it, I was past being angry, and I forgave you.'

I made no allusion to her unfinished letter. 'If I do that,' I said to myself, 'it will open up an expanse of pain she doesn't need.' I thought, 'I'll entertain her by talking instead.'

I told her about all the new things that had happened since she died.

I thought I would amuse her. I told her the story of the odd passion that had burned for three days.

'I descended on him as if by parachute. So, without any previous introduction, he found a woman, younger than he by no fewer than twenty years, standing before him and inviting him to dinner. He suppressed his surprise and embarrassment with a smile that robbed me of whatever good sense I had left. When he said, "Well then, shall we meet at such-and-such a time?" I stood on tiptoe and planted a swift kiss on his right cheek. I left him standing there rooted to the spot, and dashed to the shops. I bought a maroon silk dress. I scurried from there to a shoe shop and made my purchase: a pair of shiny black spike-heeled pumps such as you might have seen on the feet of Claudia Cardinale when she went to dinner with Marcello Mastroianni. From there I hurried to the hairdresser's salon and had my ponytail replaced with a luxuriant, shoulder-length wave. You wouldn't have recognised me! Nor did I recognise myself, for, having taken off my trousers, blouse, and trainers and put on the dress, which was sleeveless and low-cut, while my newly-styled hair covered my shoulders. I looked in the mirror, gasped, and then burst into laughter, exclaiming, "All this because of a voice?"

'I haven't told you that the seduction had been in his voice, entirely. I was sitting, just as I had sat a thousand times before, in the translation booth assigned to me. I was to translate his presentation, and I knew nothing about him but his name.

'I jumped when I heard his voice. At first it seemed to be my father's voice, but then I observed the difference between the two. This man's voice was more mellifluous – finer or stronger or deeper, or maybe it was his way of speaking that made his voice more beautiful: the rhythm of his speech, or the words themselves. I had to stay with him, doing simultaneous translation. This was quite a predicament, one I had never found myself in before. My heart beat rapidly, my palms were sweaty, and I struggled terribly to carry on translating as if nothing had happened.

'In Arabic, Mama, when we say that it was as if a bird had landed on someone's head, we are describing a person in a state of mute astonishment, caught by surprise. When I encountered him, a strange bird landed on my head, one that silenced me in his presence; I would listen, studying his face and his physiognomy. No sooner did I part company with him, though, than my strange bird stepped off my head and inhabited me, and I would fly, fly like the bird, whether I was eating, moving from one place to another, or sitting in the translation booth and doing the job I was there for.

'Three days, and then we went our separate ways. If it had been other than a fleeting encounter, there would have been an explosion.' I laughed. 'The butane gas tanks in the building might have exploded and set fire to the entire street – maybe the whole neighbourhood!' Still laughing, I added, 'I sealed

162

off the tanks and opened the windows, and, just in case, I called the fire department and kept the number for the ambulance next to the telephone!'

I told her about how I had turned down a proposal of marriage. Having sprung this on her, I clarified that I was now talking about a different man. I explained the reasons for my refusal. 'It seems you're not convinced,' I said, and proceeded to elaborate on my explanation.'

I said, 'I'm still gathering material for my book about prison. Someday I'll write it.'

I said, 'I miss you – it's strange how I miss you, because I keep thinking, as I come and go from Cairo, that here it is five years since you left and I must have got used to it. But then here I am now, next to you, and fully cognisant of my need to hold your hand – to take it and hold on as tightly as a child fearful of getting lost, utterly lost, if her hand should slip from yours.'

'Do you forgive me?' I said.

'Good night,' I said.

On the train going back, I kept blowing my nose. I was perplexed that I had told her 'Good night,' when I hadn't even noticed that the sun had gone down and dusk had fallen.

'Life is so strange,' I thought. For during this trip, which I had begun and ended by visiting my mother's grave, I had laughed with the twins, as I had never laughed in all my life.

Our sojourn in the hotel room seemed rather like a comic play, since, in order to economise, we had stayed all together in one room in a hotel in the rue des Ecoles. With regard to the space it afforded, it wasn't a bad room, but the en suite bathroom was ridiculously cramped. The toilet was right in front of the door, with no more than two or three feet of space dividing them; also, after relieving oneself, it was necessary to stand up cautiously and bend over slightly, so as not to bump one's head on the ceiling, and then to contort oneself and incline to the left before opening the door and proceeding carefully so as to avoid colliding with the sink on the right, the bathtub on the left, the toilet behind, or the half-open door in front. Then there was the matter of bathing, which called for still more advanced tactics and strategy. The bathtub was square, with space for one person to stand under the spigot, enclosed on two sides by walls and on the other two by glass panels, one of which was a door that opened only halfway (because of the position of the toilet), such that a person – provided he was not overweight, was humble before God, bowed his head, and raised and lowered his foot cautiously while getting into this square – might accomplish a bath without some frightful accident. There was no such assurance as to the next stage of the process, the business of getting out of the tub: for a section of the towel might fall into the face of the person making the attempt and obstruct his vision, or he might get water in his eyes and have trouble seeing properly. Then the unthinkable might come to pass, and the person would be lucky to do no more than stumble against the toilet, but if he wasn't so lucky he would collide with the toilet, lose his balance and bump into the glass door, which would send him careening in the direction of the washbasin.

Even with caution and practice, we couldn't help banging our heads or some part of our bodies as if it was some sort of daily toll, although the payment of it was accompanied by hilarity, laughter, and jokes. 'Everything okay?' one of us would ask another, on hearing the other's sudden exclamation. A voice, pained at first, would reply, 'Okay!' And the three of us would laugh, and then laugh some more when we tallied up the bumps and bruises. I announced, 'I'm more careful than you two – I only bumped my head three times: twice on the first day, and then the third time I was so busy singing I didn't pay attention.'

'That's a skewed analysis!' Nadeem exclaimed. 'You're the shortest and smallest of us, so you're at less risk of banging into things!'

'Every time I've gone into the bathroom,' Nadir put in, 'I've felt as though I was in a box and had to adapt myself to its shape! Yesterday, when I left you in the breakfast room and went up to use the toilet, I opened the door and stood there for five minutes calculating the space and considering my own bulk, in an attempt to come up with an idea of the ideal posture for sitting, getting up, going in, and going out. "Moving the shoulders this way," I thought, "is inadvisable, as is taking a step exceeding such-and-such a length, and when you open the door you should bend your torso to such-and-such an extent!" I told myself, "You'll make an engineer yet, my boy, unless your calculations are 'way off!" '

'And were they off?'

'Of course not. I figured it all out, and I haven't bumped into a single thing since yesterday morning! Now you two can wait and see how it goes!' Nadir went into the bathroom, and then we heard him yell, even though he made haste to flush the toilet at the same time, so as to disguise his 'Ouch!' with the sound of water gushing into the bowl.

We laughed still more when Nadir put the question to us: 'If Mama were with us, how would she sort herself out in there?'

We were rapt, picturing the situation, and designing strategies whereby Hamdiya – with her height and her substantial girth – might manage to get in and out of the bathroom.

'She'd have to leave the door open.'

'No way. She wouldn't even be able to get past it.'

'With a bit of effort she could manage it.'

'And the tub?'

'She'd have to strike that one from the agenda and settle for washing her face in the washbasin.'

'How would she do her ablutions at prayer-time? There's no space for her to raise her leg.'

'As long as she *intended* to perform the correct ablution it would be all right. Our religion is meant to enable worship, not impede it!'

This exchange was conducted with all seriousness, not even the ghost of a smile, as if we were gathering and storing our laughter, until the three of us all at once burst into manic guffaws that got us leaping to our feet and clapping hands, our own or each others'.

We laughed in that cramped room, in the glass-fronted breakfast salon that overlooked the rue des Ecoles; we laughed at the offerings of the 'Continental' breakfast which, no sooner had we finished it than Nadir demanded, 'So when can we have breakfast?' We laughed in the restaurant across from the hotel when we crossed the street to have dinner there. We laughed in the Metro, at the museums, in the street; we laughed when I told them how angry I got with my mother because of what she said to Gérard; we laughed when

166

I said, 'And what was I hoping for, anyway? That the boy would hold my hand or kiss me on the forehead when he told me goodbye?'

The twins were racing at full speed, as befits eighteen-year-old boys, and I was flying, as a matter of temperament and habit.

Chapter nineteen

An episode

N ADIR AND NADEEM ENROLLED in the College of Engineering at Cairo University. Nadir took on extra work and thus earned some money. Sometimes he tutored classmates, and other times he worked at a computer repair shop; during the summer he contracted with a private company and worked throughout the months of his holiday from nine in the morning until nine at night. He seemed happy, so I didn't interfere. Hamdiya objected that sitting in front of the computer so much was bad for his eyes – it distressed her that he had gone to an eye doctor and discovered that he needed eyeglasses. 'No one in our family,' she said anxiously, 'has had glasses: neither your father nor I, nor Nada nor Nadeem. It's because of the computer!'

Pretending to be in earnest, Nadir replied, 'I got my bad eyesight from my French grandmother!'

Nadeem enrolled in the school of architecture, as planned. He threw himself into his studies, which he loved. He did a great deal of reading in the history of art and architecture. During the summer holiday he couldn't find work, but during the summer after his third year his brother recommended that he work with him at the computer company where he himself was employed, and Nadeem agreed to this.

My relations with the twins were smooth and pleasant, and there were no problems in my relationship with Hamdiya. When we disagreed and I lost my temper with her or she talked irrationally, we would quarrel, but in general the row would be a passing thing, lasting no more than a few hours and leaving neither of us with hurt feelings.

Then came the event that broke all the rules.

I was sitting in front of the television. The programme was a talk show featuring a former prisoner I believed was a colleague of my father's. I called Hamdiya and the boys to listen to the discussion with me. The man (who was close to eighty years old by then) was recalling his fifteen years of incarceration in the military prison, as well as the Citadel, Liman Tora, and Mahariq. He didn't speak at length about torture, but rather went into detail about the improvements at Mahariq Prison: the theatre they had built, the technical workshop, the newsreels they produced, the educational sessions, the school they set up to teach literacy skills to prison guards who could not read or write, and the pictures that were drawn or engraved by artists upon the prison walls and doors.

The host asked him, 'You alluded once to the incident when a prisoner bowed his head and licked the dust – do such things really take place inside a prison?'

'Of course.'

'Did you experience this?'

'Of course.'

His face registered a calm that was unimaginable to me. Was it old age and the remoteness of the past, or wisdom attained at last?

The announcer asked him, 'Did your father cry when he saw you, a fine and promising doctor, with your hands in shackles?'

'No, he didn't cry.'

'What happened?'

'Nothing.'

'You don't remember anything of this first meeting with your father?'

'I remember that I tried to make things easier for him. I could imagine how difficult it was for him to see me with my legs in irons – there were iron shackles on both my legs. I didn't want him to keep silent, with me silent as well – I wanted to break the silence, so I began speaking lightly of the shackles. I said, "I've got used to them." I said, "And besides, we've hit on a trick that allows us to take them off when we're on our own." '

'And what did your father say?'

'He didn't say anything. Only I noticed as he was leaving . . .'

A slight tremor in his face.

'I noticed . . .'

It was difficult for him to speak, so he stopped, then tried again.

'I noticed, as he was leaving . . . I noticed that his shoulders were a bit stooped.'

The doctor hung his head. The camera moved off. I looked at the boys, unable to read their expressions. They were watching ancient history, you might say. Besides, they had no knowledge of the relationship between father and son.

I spent the night telling the boys about their father and his experience of prison. I talked at length about this, then expanded into a discussion of oppression in our country. Hamdiya did not take part in the conversation, but sat with us, listening in silence.

The following morning, as soon as the boys had left for school she said, 'Why do you talk to the children about these things? It's past and gone – why dig it up?'

Her words startled me. I said, 'First of all, because it's better that the boys know the story of their father. Second, because we talk about our country's history, and I don't want them to be like deaf people at a wedding, with no idea what's going on around them.'

'You're opening their eyes to politics, and politics is the way to perdition. I don't want them to go to prison like their father, I don't want armed security officers knocking on our door at dawn and taking them off to prison, like what happened to you.'

I smiled and said, 'Times have changed. We're in the '90s now. Don't worry – the ones getting put in prison now are the Islamists, and the boys don't have any Islamist leanings!'

What did I say to make her so angry? Her face was flushed, her voice high and shrill: 'I want the boys to concentrate on their studies and finish school in God-given safety, and I want them to live a normal life! I don't want their father's life for them – or yours!'

'Enough, Hamdiya!'

But she launched into a long, bizarre monologue on her own sacrifice and her patience with my interference in every matter large or small pertaining to the boys. 'I said to myself, "Be patient, Hamdiya, keep an open mind, Hamdiya, let God guide you, Hamdiya . . ." ' And on and on. Then she hurled her final thunderbolt: 'In the end, I am their mother, and the mother has a stronger connection to the child than a sister does – especially one who's not a full sister!'

I left the room, shouting, 'From the first moment I met you I knew instinctively that you were stupid. But I didn't know you had no manners!' I left the house, slamming the door violently behind me.

I stayed away from the house the whole day, and only returned home when it was past midnight. She had gone to bed. I kept this up for a whole week. I didn't say anything to the boys. On returning home late, I would find them studying in their room. They asked why I was out so much, and I said, 'I have some extra work for a couple of weeks.'

One night I came home and found them waiting for me. Nadeem opened the conversation. 'Mama said that you had a row, and that you're angry with her.'

I didn't respond.

'What happened?' Nadir asked.

I didn't respond.

Sometimes it happens that families quarrel, but then the waters flow once more in their regular course.

The waters didn't return to their usual course, not because we hadn't got past the words we had exchanged – we appeared to have got past them and gone back to our accustomed ways of interacting – but because the rift interposed itself all over again when the boys came home from university and talked about the student demonstrations protesting the Hebron massacre. These were the first major demonstrations to take place during the period of their university studies. (They had been in high school at the time of the student protests against the first invasion of Iraq in 1991.) Over dinner, the two boys began to tell the story of the students' rally.

'We heard that there was a demonstration,' said Nadir, 'and students began to trickle out from the College of Engineering, individually and in groups, heading for the main campus. Nadeem said he was going to join in. I said that security forces would crack down on the demonstration and we'd get nothing out of it but abuse. He left me and went out of the building, while I went to my lecture. I couldn't concentrate on what the teacher was saying, so I asked to be excused and went out to catch up with Nadeem.'

Hamdiya interrupted him. 'Nadeem, what were you doing putting yourself and your brother at risk?'

Laughing and flexing his arms to show his muscles like Popeye, Nadir continued, 'As his older brother, I wanted to protect him! The truth is, I didn't set out to participate – I meant just to look for him, but I found myself in the middle of the demonstration. I went out through the gate of the college and saw hundreds of security men with their helmets and protective gear, forming a wall to close off the passage between the university and the road leading to the Egypt Awakening statue and the Israeli embassy. I saw demonstrators surrounding the monument outside the campus, and others – a great many more demonstrators – behind the gate, which was closed. I walked toward the College of Applied Arts, so as to go back in by one of the side gates, but I found all the gates locked, and security forces surrounding the whole university. I began retracing my steps parallel to the wall, but before turning right into University Street, I decided I would jump over the wall on to the campus. I looked to my left to make sure there were no officers, and then I climbed the wall. One of the soldiers from central security saw me – a dark-skinned little chap – and he shouted at me, "That's forbidden, Effendi!"

'I smiled at him and said, "I have lectures to attend – have a good day!" And I leapt over the top, fast.

'I started looking for Nadeem among the students milling around behind the fence. The ones who were closest to the gate were trying to open it. I saw a female student climb the gate, holding on to the bars with both hands and chanting in a loud voice, while the other kids answered the chant. Then new chants rose up behind us, when a crowd from inside the campus – maybe they'd been making the rounds of the colleges – turned up and joined the students who were massing at the gate.

'The area extending inward, from the gate to the Central Celebration Hall, and lengthwise, from the College of Humanities to the Law School, was packed with demonstrators. I was searching all over for Nadeem, when the police started firing canisters of tear gas, and I found myself running with others who were fleeing. I didn't see when the students succeeded in opening the gate, or how I got to the university dormitories across the street, or how I came to be holding stones and lobbing them at the soldiers, who were pursuing us with truncheons, even though we were choking on the tear gas they had fired at us. I called out "Palestine for Arabs!" and ran; I said, "Call off the government dogs!" and threw stones; I said, "You sons of bitches!" and started to cough.'

Nadir was laughing; so was Nadeem. I was laughing (and laughter released the tears I'd been holding in ever since Nadir had begun to talk).

Nadeem spoke up. 'Nadir was under attack in University City, and I was under attack over by the Egypt Awakening statue.'

'No,' Nadir interrupted him, 'you've got that wrong, Nadeem, sir! I was under attack, but I was fighting back. I was

174

at the head of the most powerful fighting force in the Middle East!'

Hamdiya didn't laugh. Her face was pale and drawn, with a faint, bluish tinge.

It was the predicament of a mother sharing the responsibilities of motherhood. I disagreed with Hamdiya, but the split that would drive her to move out and go to live with her sister was still to come.

Chapter twenty

Hazem

At the outset, I didn't notice whether I was optimistic or pessimistic. When I heard that crow rasping in the street leading to the university, I didn't think anything, except that it was a crow. Its croak was a signal that drew my gaze upward, where I saw it sitting on a branch of one of the acacia trees lining the pavement alongside Orman Garden. Then the crow spread its wings and flew off across the street, toward the buildings of the College of Engineering, to my left. I continued on my way to the university. When my father died a few days later, I remembered the crow, and decided that it had been a sign.

'I don't believe it!'

'Believe it or don't believe it.'

'But how? Explain to me!'

'I take some things as good omens and others as evil omens; every morning I like to take a quick look at "Your fortune today" in the newspaper. I don't spend long on it, but if what it says is disturbing then I may be a bit bothered by anxiety – just a touch – until the day concludes without mishap. Anyway, we all have our quirks!'

'I've known you more than twenty-five years, and it's the first I've heard of this!'

'There was no occasion to tell you. And maybe I don't take things seriously except when I see a sign that's followed by misfortune.'

'And maybe – quite frankly, my dear *Madame* Nada, you're an idiot, and too embarrassed to admit that you're an idiot!'

'And maybe – quite frankly, my lord Hazem, sir – you take it for granted that everyone functions the same way, like the trains on the rails, so you think classification is easy: dividing people into columns, putting them on shelves and in drawers, with an original and back-up copies, and all of it identically formatted!'

He got angry, so I let him off the hook. 'I'm joking with you,' I told him. 'Weren't you joking with me, or do you actually think I'm an idiot?'

I had offered this unwarranted description of him to tease him, but I had also deceived him when I said I didn't take things seriously unless I saw a sign that was followed by misfortune. The truth was that I was always sensing ill omens. Even with things that called for rejoicing, I was fearful and driven to forebodings: that something would arise to disable or destroy or cancel whatever good thing had happened. After Arwa killed herself, I took to making daily telephone calls to a number of my friends, to see that they were all right, or ask after their close friends:

'How is so-and-so?'

'Fine.'

'Have you seen him recently?'

'Just yesterday.'

'Was he in good health?'

They made fun of me.

Or I would drop in suddenly on a friend I hadn't seen in years. I would knock on the door, and he or she would open up and cry, 'Nada!'

'I came to see if you were all right,' I would say. Hazem announced that Nada had become mother to the Egyptians, that she had decided to extend her authority in the care of her brothers to the generation as a whole!

I rang Hazem on the morning of the last day of December. 'Tomorrow,' I said, 'is the start of a new millennium. Let's spend New Year's Eve together. Who do you suggest should join us?'

'I'm not going out,' he replied.

I tried to entice him with food. 'I'll create a wonderful dish for you.'

But he wasn't interested. I didn't sense anything amiss, nor did it seem to me that there was anything worrisome in his voice. I stayed home as well. At midnight, when the new year began, I told Hamdiya good night. 'Don't stay up waiting for the boys as you usually do,' I said. 'They won't be home before morning.' And with that I went to bed.

When I learned of his death, I said, 'Oh, my God. Where am I to go now?' I put on mourning clothes and went to his house. I didn't say, nor did his mother, his brothers, or any of our comrades who had assembled at the house before the funeral, that he was a father and a companion to us, a fact which we all acknowledged yet kept to ourselves. For what was the use of saying it – what would be the point?

At the funeral, on the following day, my grief mingled with a fear such as I had never before known. I was trembling and having difficulty walking without losing my balance. Someone put his coat over my shoulders and held on to my arm throughout the funeral. At the ceremony in the great mosque two days later, Nadir and Nadeem accompanied me, and didn't leave me at the point were the men and women separate, but went with me to the section designated for the women, waiting until I was seated and a friend whom they knew had sat next to me. They went to the section reserved for the men, but Nadir came to check on me, then went back. After that Nadeem came to ask whether I needed anything. They kept on taking turns until the sheikh finished reading the verses from the Qur'an and the mourners began to disperse. They escorted me out of the mosque, and back home.

I didn't understand what was happening to me. I understood the grief over Hazem's death, but not the terror. Later, perhaps, I realised that, by some strange rationalisation, I was telling myself that it was Hazem's departure that was the portent, that the sign was not a mere crow that opened its beak to croak on a tree-branch and then flew off; rather it was the loss of Hazem, at the beginning of the year and of the century and of the millennium. 'What's to come is horrifying – what am I to do now, what will we do?' Then, too, the crow had flown off to the left, towards the College of Engineering.

I related this to Nadir and Nadeem, and began enumerating for them the names of those who had been students at the college and who had died, including founders of the organisation of supporters of the Palestinian revolution. But I didn't tell them I was frightened half to death, that I saw the grave yawning wide-open and grim. They tried to put me at ease. Nadir said I was submitting to wrongheaded nonsense: 'I understand grieving for Hazem. His death is very painful to us

179

as well, but you shouldn't compound his loss with these ghoulish speculations – absolutely not!' He looked at me with a smile, as if he was about to tease me, but then he changed tack and gave a signal to his brother. They picked me up from the bed and carried me around the house, me shouting at them to put me down while they continued with their antics. When at last they put me down, they laughed, and I laughed with them.

Normally I feel lighthearted, as if I could fly, and I do fly – really, no exaggeration. I was flying when I used to romp with the boys at home, until the neighbours complained of our commotion. I flew when we ran around at the zoo or the aquarium, the boys trying in vain to catch up with me. I would fly – however strange this may seem – while settled in a chair reading a good novel, or translating a beautiful passage, or inventing a dish no one had ever thought of or put in a cookbook, or when I would roar out a song in the shower, noisily destroying the melody, accompanied by the sound of rushing water as it sprayed my head and body. I recall now, too, that throughout the two years during which I partici-pated in the student movement, I would fly to the university, fly to the sit-in, fly to the demonstration.

When I find myself feeling heavy, I know I'm on the brink of a new bout of depression. I told the doctor who was treat-ing me, 'I have guilt feelings I can't get rid of. I feel guilty toward my father and toward my mother – guilty feelings there's no cure for, because they've died. And I feel guilty every time one of my comrades dies, as if I had left him or her to bear a burden I didn't share. I'm aware of the contradiction in what I'm saying, but this is how I feel. Or maybe my words are an illusion I spin because the truth is that I feel guilty every time I look around and realise we're leaving a mess for the younger generation and expecting them to live in it.'

'I'm afraid,' I tell the doctor, 'awake or asleep. Maybe I rush around because I'm afraid, and rushing around alleviates my fear – I'm no longer aware of it. When fear takes over I find myself unable to get up or to walk. I huddle in bed. Going to work or leaving the house seems an impossible task. I am as afraid as I can be of going out. I'm afraid of people, and at the same time I feel desolate because I'm removed from them. The moment when I wake up is the hardest. It takes me two hours to get ready to leave for work, not because I'm preening and grooming myself, but because I'm incapable of going out to the street, going to my job, and meeting whoever it is I may meet. When I do go to work, and absorb myself in it, the fear recedes as if it had been a dream, or as if the state I was in in the morning had been nothing but phantasms and illusions. I've called my feelings "fear", but I'm not sure whether that's an accurate description. Maybe it's something else – weariness, or anxiety, or a mixture of feelings of which fear is only one component. I don't know.'

He listens without interrupting, except with brief interjections. When I stop talking, he asks me whether I am able to get my work done. 'Sometimes I have trouble concentrating,' I say 'but on the whole I have no difficulty at work. Translation isn't a problem for me. I can do simple translation quickly and automatically; it is the more difficult type of translation, of literary and theoretical texts – the kind I usually enjoy and in which I find a kind of challenge or stimulating entertainment – that I don't go near. If I'm tired, I don't sign on for that kind of translating – or if I've already made a commitment, I set it aside and don't honour my commitment.'

The doctor asserts that I am stronger than I think. He says my defences are strong. I don't believe him, and am sceptical about the usefulness of these long, costly sessions. I leave his clinic and walk in the street, weeping. I dry my tears and go into the chemist's to pick up my prescription. I take the medication conscientiously for two or three days, then toss it in the bin. I don't need medication!

It is essential that I unravel the threads – surely I will find a way out. What is the problem? I must identify the problem before trying to solve it. What is the problem?

Chapter twenty-one

The big feast

S OMETIMES I AM VISITED by my good angel, and at such times I think there is much to life that makes it worth living. I remember the moments that shone brightly, and conclude that the world, in spite of everything, has been kind to me.

When Nadir and Nadeem turned sixteen, I suggested we have a party to celebrate. We weren't in the habit of giving birthday parties; it was enough to wish 'many happy returns' to the person whose birthday it was, or perhaps mark the event with a bouquet of flowers, a card, or a shirt whose purchase was urged by the occasion.

We didn't hold the party on the day itself, but rather some days afterward, when the boys came home, each with his identity card confirming that he had officially become a full and independent citizen. 'Friday evening?' I suggested, and they agreed. I spent Thursday night and Friday morning preparing the sweets. Then I announced, 'The kitchen is closed – no spongers admitted!' This was in reference to Nadir and Nadeem, for Hamdiya had worked with me on the preparations. I took a bath and let down my hair, which I normally kept tied back in a ponytail. I put on my prettiest outfit. The guests arrived and the party became a feast. We sang, danced, played, laughed, and made fun, words flying all around like ping-pong balls in games of repartee, with jokes and sarcastic jibes targeting everything, not least of all ourselves.

When the boys graduated with their high school baccalaureate, we held a second celebration, and we had a third when they graduated from the university. At the end of every celebration I would go to bed – or to put it more accurately, I would drop into bed like a sack of onions or potatoes tossed from a transport lorry. I would sink into a deep and peaceful sleep, while the party continued until the next morning. As soon as I awoke, I would hurry to the bathroom, run the hot water and take a long, leisurely bath, the steam thick around me, while I sang my heart out, songs I loved by Fayrouz or Abdel Wahhab.

My feelings were similar to this on that sweltering day in July when I said goodbye to the boys at the Cairo airport, and if I hadn't been too shy I would have raised up my voice and belted out the song I was singing in an undertone and the airport would have come to a stop in consternation at this woman past the age of forty (it might not have seemed to the casual observer that I was over forty, because of my clothes and the arrangement of my hair tied back in a ponytail, but I had reached the age of forty-six – or, in classical Arabic, I was 'a woman in the fifth decade of her life', having covered more than half the distance between the fifth and the sixth) – I say, had I *vociferated* in song (this word 'vociferate' is one of the more unfortunate specimens of our beautiful language), the airport would have come to a stop in consternation at such bizarre behaviour, perhaps also at my exceptional ability to reduce any melody to a discordant cacophony. At any rate, I carried on singing in a low voice as I handed over my passport to the Middle East Airlines employee, and then I stopped, perforce, to answer her question. 'I only have this one small bag with me,' I said, 'and I'll carry it on.' I took my passport, went back to singing, and continued singing as I stood in the queue for passport security, held out the passport for the officer to administer the exit stamp, and finally as I settled into a seat at the airport café, to wait for departure.

I had followed the drama minutely, every day, every hour. The first day, I sat watching the television from the time I got home from work until evening. On the second day, I dashed to work, did what was required of me, and dashed back home. For the next two days I didn't leave the house or my spot in front of the television. To begin with, there was the liberation of Qantara, Deir Seriane, Al-Qsair, and Taibe. Then more villages and towns followed: Markaba, Beit Yahoun, Al-Adaisse, Al-Houla, Beni Haiyane, Tallouse, Meiss al-Jabal, Kfar Kila, Al-Khiam, Al-Naqoura, Bent Jbail, Marj'oyun. I corroborated the events by going back to the map, to ascertain the location of each. In a matter of days, these villages and towns, previously unknown to me, became places that were intimately familiar. When Nadir and Nadeem got home from work, I would recount to them the details of what I had seen; after naming each village and town, I would point out its specific location. Suddenly I laughed, remembering my aunt, when she talked about the villages neighbouring ours – how she took great care to say just where they were: on the land to the east or the land to the west, bordering our village or some other place; and the distance between the two: as if she feared that her listener would mistake the location of our village and lose his way.

The Israeli army had fled.

A desperate attempt on the part of Lahad's men. Bombardment of the people of Bent Jbail returning to their hometown. Another attempt: The Israelis opened fire and struck their own agents in Lahad's army. A third attempt: They poured petrol from the tanks onto the roads. No use. At Al-Shaqif, the last fortified position in which they had a presence, a group was besieged, waiting to be airlifted by helicopter to Israel. Then the collapse – complete and final collapse. They left behind their tanks, transport vehicles, heavy artillery, rifles, pistols, ammunition, and an army of their agents.

It would be very difficult for me to describe my feelings as I followed the thousands of people setting out for their liberated villages, making their way along dusty tracks, climbing the hills either on foot, or by car or motorcycle. Yellow flags, green flags, and flags of a white background coloured with green and red. Bulldozers removing the barriers. The gate that had closed off the road to them opened by hands, arms, and shoulders. The people passed through, and kept on ascending, getting closer, reaching their destination: women strewed the new arrivals with rice and rose petals. *Ahlan wa sahlan!* Welcome home! 'Twenty years we've been dead, and now we are reborn.' These words were spoken by an old man as he greeted the new arrivals. A woman wearing an army uniform was asked by another who was there with the media whether the uniform was part of 'the spoils of victory'. 'No,' she replied, 'these clothes belonged to a comrade of my son – both of them martyrs.'

'Are you happy on this day?' the journalist asked her.

The woman replied, 'Happy, yes, but my happiness will be complete when the detainees come back from the Israeli prisons, and the bodies of our martyred sons are returned to us.'

A youth pulled down a poster displaying a picture of one of the leaders of the collaborating army, tore it to pieces, and continued on his way. Young girls wept, women ululated and sang, two men embraced and held the embrace for a long time, as if afraid that if one of them let go of the other he might find his friend behind barbed wire that would once again keep them apart. In a dusty village square, a prayer was held that united those returning with those who had stayed on in the village. A group photograph of the residents of Bent Jbail, taken in front of the town's telephone company, which had been the collaborators' headquarters, laughing faces, people pressed shoulder-to-shoulder, yellow flags fluttering, in a still shot, as if addressing time itself: 'Take this picture – document this.'

The men of Lahad's army, which had collaborated with Israel, gave themselves up. The camera moved in on them as they sat in a large transport vehicle. They hid their faces. The jig was up. Their leaders had asked permission to take refuge with their families in Israel. A long line of people and cars stood awaiting permits to cross. The Fatima Gate closed behind the last Israeli soldier leaving Lebanon – the television showed the great iron gate and broadcast the loud creaking noise it made as its two panels swung on their hinges. An Israeli soldier on the other side encircled it with heavy chains. Then the iron lock.

At Bent Jbail, Hasan Nasrallah said in his speech on the twenty-sixth of May, 2000, 'Put away your despair. Arm yourselves,' he said, 'with hope.'

Antoine Lahad, in a statement from Paris, said, 'We dedicated ourselves to Israel for twenty-five years, but Israel betrayed and abandoned us in a single night.'

Nasrallah said in his speech, 'The age of defeat is over.'

The next day (the twenty-seventh of May), I got out of bed the moment I awoke, took a shower, and put on a brightly coloured dress – it was the first time I had shed mourning garb since Hazem's death. I made myself a cup of tea, picked up a pen, and sat down to write to him:

'Couldn't you have held on for five months? You only needed to wait four months and twenty days – no more – and then your life would have gone on for years. I miss you so much, but I'm going to set that aside now and tell you what's happened.' And I told the story, told in detail what I had seen via live television broadcast; then I drew a map for him showing the locations of the villages and towns. At the end of the letter, I told him that I meant to visit southern Lebanon as soon as I got the chance. (Hazem was the first person I told of my travel plans.) When I finished the letter, I put it in an envelope, but when I went to write the address, I felt perplexed; I put the letter in my handbag, and got up to make myself another cup of tea and get ready for work.

It seemed to me for a moment that I might continue writing letters to Hazem. I told myself that this could be the beginning of one of my sudden manias. Or it could be true madness, the kind that would remove me from the rational world. But I wrote him only one more letter after that, which I began when I was at Beirut Airport, waiting for my flight. I continued writing on the plane. When I finished this letter, the flight attendant was telling us to fasten our safety belts, because the plane was about to land at Cairo Airport.

In my letter to Hazem I told him about the road to the town of Al-Khiam, about the colour photographs of young men that were to be found along the way: 'At every position

188

where there had been an operation by the resistance was a pole – like a lamp-post, only instead of being topped by a light it bore a picture of a martyr who took part in the operation: a large colour photograph in which the facial features stood out clearly, and underneath the picture was the young man's name, with the date and the year in which he was martyred.'

I told him about the prison at Al-Khiam: its location overlooking Palestine and Syria and Mount Amil in Lebanon. I described it to him minutely, beginning with the list hung on the left side of the entrance to the courtyard: a record of all the gaolers who had engaged in torture. I described to him the interrogation chamber, the 'hanging rod', the large cells and the small ones – these were one square metre and not quite two metres in height, where a prisoner would spend a month or two with no opportunity to stretch out or to extend his legs fully. I said, 'I went into one of them and pushed the door shut – I couldn't see my hand in front of my face, in the gloom.' I told him about the box: A prisoner would sit cross-legged in there for days, in a space whose dimensions measured one cubic metre. I told him about the exercise yard in the sun, roofed with barbed wire, where prisoners were allowed to go for twenty minutes once every three weeks. The prison was left as it was after liberation, to become a museum for visitors, but the walls were repainted, and so we lost everything that had been written or inscribed or drawn on them. There was nothing, now, on the walls.

I did not tell him what I had heard about the various kinds of torture, or the breakouts that had been attempted despite the minefield encircling the prison, but I related in detail two of the many stories I had heard: the tale of Ali Qashmar, who had spent ten years in the prison, and that of Abdallah Hamza, who had stayed there only three weeks.

'Ali was from the town of Al-Khiam. They arrested him when he was fourteen years old. He didn't know what the charge was. He said, "I was like other boys my age: I hated the occupation, but all I thought about was fun and games. I wasn't much concerned with the future, and if I did think about it, then my thoughts went no further than the hope that I would pass my examinations."

'He was arrested and tortured, tortured extensively.

'His mother went up to the roof of her house every day. She gazed toward the buildings of the nearby prison and talked to her son, as if her words might reach him, as if he would respond to the things she told him. The neighbours would hear her, and gently bring her back down from the roof.

'When he got out of prison, his mother didn't recognise him. In her mind he was a small boy, and standing before her was a tall young man with a beard. Smiling, he said to her, "Mother, it's me, Ali!"

'She knew him by his smile.

'He, too, failed to recognise himself one day when he looked at himself in the mirror in the guard's room. He said, "Reflected in its surface I saw someone I didn't know. I turned to look behind me, but found no one.

' "I had spent ten years in prison. The teacher Abdallah Hamza, on the other hand, was there only three weeks. They hung him on the 'hanging rod' and kept beating him and pouring cold water on him (this was in February) until he died. For two and a half years Fayrouz, his wife and the mother of his three children, continued to visit the prison, travelling the fifty kilometres from her village to Al-Khiam, bringing her husband clothes and food, which she would leave with the guard and then go home. For two and a half years she was unaware that she was a widow; unaware, for two and a half years, that her children were fatherless."

'The stories of Ali Qashmar and Abdallah Hamza were told to me by the guide who conducted me through the prison. He, too, was a former prisoner. He did not tell me his own story. He spoke of himself only as one member of a larger group, as he led me from cell to cell, from the interrogation chambers to the "hanging rod", explaining everything, exhaustively.'

At the end of the letter, I told Hazem, 'In my book about prison, I'll devote a chapter to Al-Khiam, which, unlike the other chapters, will discuss the moment of liberation. Perhaps I'll devote two chapters to it – one to be the focal point in a book about life in prison, and the other, with which I'll conclude, on liberation.'

Chapter twenty-two

Novelty

NADIR WAS TRAINING ME to use the computer. I found it confusing, and felt completely stupid at first, then less so. I groped my way as timidly as someone taking up a pen for the first time, or someone expected to be responsive in a language of which he has learned only the rudiments. Losing patience, I would say, 'I get it now. Let me figure it out.' He would leave me alone to flounder for a bit, and then I would call for help, demanding explanations every few minutes. Nadir would come and sort me out, but he would overdo the explanation, going on and on until I protested, 'What, do you think I'm an idiot?' He would go away again, and things would seem simpler for a bit, then get complicated again. Then I would summon Nadeem.

For the first week, working with the programmes and files and windows and message boxes that jumped on to the screen in front of me – to which I didn't know whether I should answer 'Yes' or 'No' – I felt I was wandering a maze in the streets of an unknown city. I would stop. Then I would make up my mind and say, 'This is the way,' and proceed with some degree of confidence, but this would gradually fade, until I became convinced that I was simply lost, with no idea how to get to where I wanted to go, or how to go back the way I had come. I said, 'Teach me how to work with just the documents.' I was good at writing quickly on the keyboard; now I wanted to learn how to open a new document, how to close it, how to get back to it, and how to organise what I'd written and edit text by adding to it or cutting from it. He taught me.

The following day, I opened a new document, and began translating. I put the text on my right and looked at the Arabic sentences, moving my fingers easily on the keyboard, as the French sentences took shape on the screen before me. I usually translated quickly, and as a rule I would go back over the draft of what I had translated at the end of each paragraph. Now the emendation process was simpler and faster: I could delete a letter or a word or a line and substitute another. No need to draft text only to white it out and then go back to it for the final adaptation, to be copied for the third time. I worked assiduously on the document for four days, during which I translated fifty pages.

I was happy, as I generally was, when my translation of a text pleased me, and happier still about my success in working with a device that, only one week earlier, had seemed like an insoluble puzzle.

What had happened? Some keystroke resulting in some action or other. The document had disappeared. For two hours, I tried to get it back, but I got nowhere. I was certain it was hiding somewhere in the depths of the machine, so I sat waiting for one or the other of the boys to return and find it.

Nadir came home and as usual declared that he was starving to death, that if he didn't eat immediately we would have to summon an ambulance, and that before the ambulance could get there the doctor would have pronounced him dead!

I took him by the hand and sat him down before the computer. 'The document first,' I told him, 'and then you can perish at your leisure, I won't stop you!' Hamdiya stared, astonished, but held her tongue.

Nadir sat at the computer and asked me the name of the document, the date it was created, and the last time I had worked on it. He searched. 'It's not there,' he said. Then his fingers began a series of rapid clicks on the mouse. Boxes and lists appeared, while he indicated 'no' or 'yes', closing this, opening that, closing the other. At last he announced, 'I have a right to eat now. I worked for my snack. You've lost the document, Miss Nada!'

'That can't be! How did it go missing?'

'You must have needed to press "save", but . . .'

'What do you mean, "press 'save'"?'

'That means you preserve the document. That's computer-ese: "Saving" means preserving your work.'

'And?'

'The document got lost because you shut down the computer without saving it.'

'That's not what happened.'

'Then tell me what happened. But let me eat first, and then I'll listen.'

I sat next to him while he had his dinner. I told him, 'The power went out, and the computer turned off. Then the power came back, I turned it on, and the document was there – no problem. I worked on it for four hours, and when I decided to stop the message box for me to save it came up, so I pressed "Yes" as usual, and the same box came up a second time, and then a third and a fourth. I did the same thing twenty times, then decided that the "Yes" button was useless.

It seemed as though pressing "No" would solve the problem, so that's what I did. After that I closed the document, shut down the computer, and went into the kitchen. Then this afternoon when I turned it on I couldn't find the document.'

'Brilliant! Fantastic! I've got to hand it to you, by God! When the electricity went out, the computer saved a temporary copy of the document. You simply had to change its name or save it with the same name by substituting the temporary document with a permanent one. Every time you gave the "save" command, the computer was waiting for you to tell it under what name you wanted the document saved. What you were supposed to do was . . .'

I wasn't listening anymore. I was thinking about how I had lost four days' worth of work.

'From now on,' I announced, 'I'm not going anywhere near the computer.'

Nadir shook his head, shrugged, and said, to goad me, ' "Scared to get into the water, Nadir? Shame on you!" '

He was mimicking what I used to say to him when he was little and fearful of swimming.

When Nadeem came back, Nadir turned the loss of the document into a stage comedy.

'I come home and find Nada raising a lament, wailing, "My document, my document!" I tell her I'm about to die of hunger. "My document, my document!" she says. The telephone rang, and she answered it, "My document, my document!" There was a knock on the door. It was a grocery delivery-man. She said, "My document, my document!" '

For weeks I didn't go near the computer. Then one Friday after breakfast the boys pulled me over to the machine and sat down, one on either side of me and each with a newspaper.

'We're not moving,' they said. 'Turn on the computer and work with it.' Every time I tried to move from my place they prevented me. Finally I said, 'I want to go to the toilet.' They didn't believe me. 'I swear,' I told them, but they still didn't believe me. I said to them, 'Look, lads, I'll work on my own!' They let me go. They stood by the bathroom door, and shouted, one after the other, 'That's it!' And they dragged me back from the door of the bathroom to the computer.

Then the new plaything caught hold of me. It took hold even more firmly when I learned how to use e-mail and surf the Internet. I could follow the news, read the papers and the magazines, and look for whatever I wanted to know on one subject or another.

One glorious morning I announced, like a cock crowing, 'News of the hour: I've now got my own blog!' The boys shouted as if the team they were cheering for had scored a goal – they clapped and cheered.

'What's your blog called?'

' "Mendicant dervish." '

'Beautiful!' said Nadeem.

But Nadir retorted, 'That's pathetic. Think of another name.'

'Such as?'

' "Aziza, the sultan's daughter," Or,' he added, ' "Princess Qatr al-Nada" – dewdrop, like the meaning of your name.'

' "Mendicant dervish," ' said Nadeem. 'It's beautiful – if you decide to change it, make it "I wonder".'

'I'll leave it the way it is!'

Hamdiya disliked the computer. She felt it had taken Nadir away from her, then Nadeem, and then I, too, started putting in long sessions in front of it. The boys and I would often find ourselves absorbed in conversation that made her feel left out, since she didn't understand what we were talking about. She kept saying that the computer wasted time and strained the eyes. Days went by when I didn't enter the kitchen at all, and I noticed how tense she was when she set the table. Rather than put the plates, forks, and knives down calmly, she banged them down with a clatter loud enough to jangle my ears, even in the next room.

I resumed my quarrel with Hamdiya when Nadir applied for, and was offered, a job in Dubai. I was amazed when she rejoiced at the news. I objected. 'You like your work,' I said to him, 'and you earn good wages by it.' I tried to talk him round, but he maintained that the job that had been offered to him would afford him mobility within his field, broader experience, a bigger salary, and higher status.

He'd made up his mind, and he went abroad.

We were in touch every night by e-mail, but it seemed that Nadir had a great deal of work in hand, so his communications were brief, except on Thursdays and Fridays. He seemed to be happy with his job, and with the large salary he was earning.

Nadeem had no luck finding a job. All the architectural engineering firms gave preference to those with experience, and he couldn't find a job that would provide him with such experience: a catch-22. He moved around from one job to another in private computer firms. He enrolled in a graduate programme, hoping that if he got a master's degree in architecture it would improve his chances of work in his field.

The firm he had left allowed him time for his academics, but was late in paying its employees. Nadeem would receive his pay packet in the latter half of the month, or at the end of the month, or sometimes the following month. They would say they were waiting for some cheque to come through before they could pay their wages. 'This is a small firm?' I asked him. He said, 'No, it's a large firm, with hundreds of employees. The owners know we need work, and they know that the number of qualified candidates is limitless. If one of us leaves, there's a queue of thousands of unemployed people looking to take his place. They put it bluntly: "Nobody's forcing you to stay." '

The new firm he transferred to paid wages regularly, and therefore squeezed him hard, like juicing a sugar cane. He would leave the house at seven-thirty in the morning and come home at one o'clock in the morning, every day, six days a week. He would come in like a sleepwalker, eat his meal in a semi-somnolent state, then go to bed. (Had Marx been alive, he would have added a new observation regarding the surplus value produced by university-educated white-collar workers. I wonder how he would classify them: as a middle class, or a toiling workforce?)

Fridays were my only opportunity to communicate with Nadeem. We would have a leisurely breakfast and stay seated at the kitchen table, chatting and at ease. He would tell me about his co-workers and their situations, and about what he saw on the microbus he took back and forth to work. (It took him more than an hour to get to work – an hour and a quarter or an hour and a half each way.)

Months went by, and Nadeem said to me, 'The driver used to play a recording of Qur'anic recitation. The volume was turned up high and reverberated throughout the bus, but it didn't stop the passengers talking. They made their comments, and gossiped, and told their stories, sometimes making fun.

198

No one tells jokes now. Lately a strange thing has come about: The driver doesn't play recordings and none of the passengers talk – silence has fallen on the microbus, everyone is lost in his own thoughts – it's as if a bird had landed on everyone's head. That's what I've observed on the different microbuses I take every day. But the strangest thing I've noticed is that if the passengers do talk – which happens only rarely now – if one person speaks and another answers, then conversation breaks out, and people talk provocatively about politics, and in stronger terms than you can imagine. Their criticism touches on everything, from the price of bread to government corruption to the gunboats moving in to strike Iraq.'

Nadir surprised us with an unannounced visit. There was a knock on the door Thursday evening, and there we found him. He had a small case in his hand, with another smaller bag slung from his shoulder. The commotion of our reunion was followed by mad excitement, as we hugged him one after another, with Hamdiya weeping, me laughing, Nadir talking, and Nadeem emitting odd sounds, so it was as if a flock of birds were fluttering and squawking and singing. Nadir announced, 'First of all, this is one of those visits of the kind that go, "Is so-and-so with you? No? Then I'll be on my way." '

'You mean one week?'

'Thursday, Friday, and then Saturday morning I'm off.'

'No!'

Nadir continued, 'The reason for this visit is Nada's birthday. I said to myself, "This is the first birthday with me a solid working man earning a solid wage." '

With that he set upon me, kissed me on both cheeks and on my forehead. 'Happy birthday,' he said, 'and many happy returns – you're the best!' He handed me the bag that had been hanging from his shoulder since he appeared on the doorstep. 'Open it.'

I did so. I didn't say a word, for I couldn't have uttered a sound without shedding tears. Nadir understood me, and didn't prolong the moment. He turned to Hamdiya. From his jacket pocket he drew a small box, opened it, and presented her with an elegant little watch. She wept some more. He said, 'As for Nadeem, he'll have to wait until the next visit, since my salary goes only so far. I bought two shirts, one for you and one for myself.'

Within seconds, the boys had taken off their shirts and begun taking the wrapping off the new ones, pulling out the pins and plastic collar-pieces, and undoing the buttons. Each donned his new shirt – the two garments were identical. Then Nadir announced, 'If I don't eat straightaway, I'm going to die and miss the chance to go out in my new shirt!'

'Didn't you eat on the plane?'

'I ate, but only Hamdiya and Nada's food can fill me up!'

The four of us stood in the kitchen, as I fixed one dish and Hamdiya another, while Nadeem made a salad, and Nadir told us his news. Then we carried the plates to the dining table. We stayed at the table talking and drinking tea until the call to prayer at dawn. Only then did we go to bed.

By seven I had drunk my tea and turned on the laptop computer that Nadir had given me. It was gorgeous, magnificent. I wasn't sure whether I would have found it so beautiful had I seen it displayed for sale in some shop. 'It's beautiful because it's a gift,' I said to myself, 'and beautiful in its own right, irrespective of other considerations.' It was small, light, and elegant, its cover, the borders around the screen and the keyboard all of a fine silver colour. The keyboard was black, imprinted with Arabic and Roman letters in white. Its case was elegant as well, with one space for the machine, another for papers, and a third for storing the cords, adapter, and accessories, as well as two pockets: a square one for the compact discs that came with the computer, and another rectangular one for the mouse.

I was fixing another cup of tea when Nadeem woke up, kissed me, and shyly held out his hand, in which was something wrapped in coloured paper. 'Happy birthday, Nada,' he said.

'Thank you, sweetheart,' I replied.

'The gift doesn't measure up to the occasion.'

I opened it, kissed it, and kissed him.

We sat down to have tea together.

I was about to say, 'The laptop Nadir brought me is a treasure,' and then I thought better of it.

'By the way, Nada,' said Nadeem, 'tell Mama that you commissioned Nadir to buy you that computer.'

'But I didn't commission him!'

'I know. But it seems she's upset. Yesterday while we were fixing tea she let slip a comment that gave her away.'

'What did she say?'

'It doesn't matter what she said, but apparently she knows what that kind of equipment costs, and maybe she was comparing that to the price of the watch.'

'And why are you passing this on to me?' (The sharpness of the one-time child-rearer had resurfaced.)

'I'm not passing anything on to you. I just wanted to prevent the possibility of any misunderstanding or hurt feelings. Tell her you gave him money for the computer, that it turned out not to be enough, and he made up his mind to cover the rest of the cost. That is, a compromise between a gift and something you asked him to get for you. She'll calm down if you tell her that.'

'I won't do it!'

Then I added with finality, 'I hope Nadir won't hear about any of this nonsense!'

He was quiet. Then he said, 'Nadir suggested I go to Dubai.'

'Did you get a job offer?'

'No, but he says he'd be able to get me a job with a decent salary. What do you think?'

'What do *you* think?'

'I don't know. But if things go on like this I'm going to take him up on it.'

It's strange how we react. I took out my anger on Nadeem, not Hamdiya. I was furious with him for telling me what his mother had said – or rather, what was worse, passing along his own version of what she had said. From the time they were small, I refused to listen if Nadir said, 'Nadeem did such-and-such,' or if Nadeem said, 'Nadir said such-and-such.' I would give them a good scolding, and sometimes even punish the informer. Nadeem wasn't being an informer. He was trying, pointlessly, to avert hurt feelings. Did he avert them or create them? Nadir was to be with us just one day; there was nothing for it but for me to drop the whole subject as if I hadn't heard anything of it. But how?

Over lunch, Nadir said to me, 'You look pale, Nada.'

'I overate last night, and slept only two hours. Besides, we've started the countdown – you're leaving tomorrow.'

'Let's think of today, not tomorrow. Nadeem and I are going to make you a birthday cake, whether it gets eaten or not – it's the thought that counts.'

'I'll make it,' Hamdiya put in.

I said, 'I'm inviting you all to lunch at a restaurant – there's no need for a cake. Thank you, Hamdiya.'

Chapter twenty-three

Blue lorries

S OMETHING NEW WAS HAPPENING that struck me as odd, and I couldn't let it go. I was following the blue lorries – I would encounter them by chance on the road, and pursue them. I said nothing about this to anyone, as my behaviour might provoke ridicule or at least laughter, or doubts as to my mental health. I would catch sight of them two or three cars ahead of me, or notice that they were behind me when they were reflected in the car's rear-view mirror, or one of the side mirrors. I would find myself spontaneously turning the wheel to the right or left, speeding up or slowing down, jockeying for a place next to them. Most of the time I would be prevented by the heavy traffic in the streets and squares, or a light would turn red suddenly, forcing me to stop, or else a green light would oblige me to move forward inopportunely, or a couple of cars might pass me and I would fail to catch up with them. Sometimes there was a fork in the road, and my day's agenda (if I was on my way to work or to an appointment I couldn't miss) wouldn't permit me to follow them, since I might end up where I hadn't meant to go, deep in the byways from which it would take me more time than I had to extricate myself.

They were big vehicles, of a hue that was nothing like either sky-blue or sea-blue, but the raw blue of cheap paint to which dust had clung until it became part of it. Perhaps the surface had been repainted over and over, without being cleaned or sanded first, so that the last layer of colour went on muddy and uneven. The driver and the one or two men beside him were all from the rank and file of the police force. Behind them would be the big iron box, with a door at the rear and a set of steps between that and the street. The door would be locked with a large deadbolt and sometimes a padlock in addition to that. In rare cases a couple of boys would be standing there – boys from the countryside in uniforms that were filthy, albeit official – as auxiliary security guards. On either side of the box, in the upper third portion, were four small openings close together, presumably windows, with iron bars or instead of bars some thick metal grillwork that would restrict the airflow for whoever was inside the box and limit the visibility of those behind these openings, keeping them that much more tightly in bonds.

They were called 'transport lorries', for they were used to convey those who had been arrested from one place to another – from the police department, for example, or from the public prosecutor's office to the courtroom and from there to prison.

When I followed one of these vehicles my first concern was to find out whether there were people in the box, and whether they were pressing their faces to the metal grillwork seeking a breath of air or a beam of light or some hope in the sight of a face or a tree or a school door opening suddenly for a group of children.

Having got close enough, I liked to stop my car altogether, so that the necessity of watching the road would not prevent me from staring at those windows secured with grillwork, where I might see a face, or intercept a glance or a smile. Then the urgent honk of a car horn would compel me to avert my gaze, to discover that I was on the point of colliding with the car ahead of me, or that my car was rolling backward and about to hit the one behind me.

I rarely succeeded in overtaking a transport lorry. The two or three times I was lucky, I imagined that I saw a face behind the opening, and I looked intently at it. It seemed to me that it stared at me as well. I would smile. After that, I would have no chance, because of the need to concentrate on the road, to see any response to my smile; then the vehicle would move off, and I would continue on my way.

It didn't occur to me, when I thought about this new mania that had beset me, that it was a premonition, and that my heart was anticipating what was to happen. I thought my new mania was some residue of the past, that perhaps unconsciously I was remembering my father, and following paths he might have travelled.

It didn't occur to me that the lorry was the harbinger of an evil event. Maybe I came close to thinking along these lines, and then reconsidered, wondering, 'How could this be a bad omen, when the only thing that's new is that I'm the one who's taken to following the lorries? There's no omen here, no basis for foreboding or dread. It's odd behaviour, but, whatever obscure impulses it may suggest, it's just another of my passing obsessions, nothing more.'

No more friends of mine died on New Year's Eve, nor did I see a crow making auguries toward the College of

Engineering. Nothing out of the ordinary occurred. That is to say, I spent the night in front of the computer, and then, at a polite quarter of an hour before midnight, I moved to the sitting room, where Hamdiya was watching television, and sat down with her. When the clock struck twelve, announcing the end of the year 2002, I said to her, 'Happy New Year, Hamdiya,' and kissed her. She kissed me back, and said, 'Happy New Year.' Then the phone rang, and it was Nadir ringing us from Dubai; this was followed by another call, from Nadeem, who was spending the evening with his friends.

'What would you say to a cup of mint tea, Hamdiya?'

'What an excellent idea!'

I made tea and arranged some pieces of cake on a plate with two sprigs of fresh mint and then on the side I added a handful of almonds and raisins. The plate looked pretty – smiling, I brought the tray to Hamdiya and placed it before her. 'Chef Nada,' I said, 'wishes you a nice night and a happy year!'

Hamdiya laughed and replied, 'You really have style, Nada!'

'A little treat on New Year's Eve!'

We drank our tea and ate the sweets, and it seemed as though the new year, like our shared company that night, would be calm, routine, perhaps pleasant.

That is not what happened.

The first two months of the new year brought cares and troubles that were only the preamble, the dry-run, for what the third month would bring.

Nadeem said that he was going to move to Dubai to work. Despite the care he took over completing his paperwork, and even though he received a travel visa for the Emirates and signed a contract with the same firm for which his brother worked, he didn't seem happy. He didn't express whatever was going on inside his head, although it was not difficult for me to read the look in his eyes. His decision to travel meant that he had to accept the way things were and resign himself to them. He wanted to study architecture, and he did; he applied himself seriously and conscientiously to his studies, acquiring knowledge that pleased him, and the door of his imagination had opened on to a dream he must now relinquish – raise a white flag before the age of thirty, and admit, 'I give up.'

In the background beat the drums of war, another war, bigger than all the rest. We followed the Security Council debates, and the unfolding scenarios of imminent conflict. 'They're going to attack Iraq,' Nadeem said, while I clung to the possibility that it was just scare tactics, an attempt at verbal terrorism. The memory of the previous war was as present as if more than ten years hadn't elapsed since then, the first war that the boys had been old enough to pay attention to. In 1982 they had been little, more preoccupied with football games, the cartoons on television, a half-point more or less on a test at school, or a goal scored in a game in which a girls' team had defeated the boys. On that day I confined myself to telling them that Israel, which had attacked us in 1956 and 1967, was attacking Lebanon. I wouldn't have approved of their watching the news broadcasts with me, and when the occupation forces moved into Beirut, with the ensuing massacre, I summarised what had occurred in an expurgated statement: 'The Israelis have been behind the killing of a great many people – when you're a little older, you'll learn how terrible Israel is.' I concealed from them, though, the videotape I had acquired, about the massacres at Sabra and Shatila

– images of bloated corpses and flies. I also concealed the elaborate tale of the Phalangists and the Lebanese forces that had perpetrated the slaughter as Israel's proxies. I thought, 'Two little boys not eight years old – why poison their imaginations with images of bloodshed, the complicated relationship between invading forces supported by locals, and a resistance supported by part of the populace, while the other part wants to crush it?'

But on the day of the first attack on Baghdad, in 1991, they were in high school, and they followed the reports on television, read the daily newspapers, and discussed the course of events with their schoolmates, agreeing or disputing.

This war now looming over Iraq would be Nadir and Nadeem's second war, and the second one to affect their lives.

Four days before the war began, there was a telephone call from one of my former classmates. 'Siham died,' the caller said.

I was about to ask him, 'Who is Siham?'

I must have been quiet a long time, for he thought the line had been disconnected. 'Hello? Hello?' he said.

'Siham Sabri?'

'Yes.'

'When?'

'Three days ago. Her obituary appeared in yesterday's *Al-Ahram*.'

'Was it suicide?'

'I don't know.'

'What does her family say?'

'They're saying she was struck by a car. We want to organise a ceremony for her. We want to publish a collective obituary in the newspaper in all our names, and we want . . .'

I rang off.

I went back to the previous day's newspaper. The announcement appeared at the top of the obituary page, in the third column from the right.

Siham died on Thursday the thirteenth of March 2003, corresponding to the tenth of Muharram in the year 1424 of the Islamic calendar. She was struck by a car in a place not very far from her home near the flyover exit to Orouba Street, which leads to the airport. Was she walking along distractedly when she crossed the road — was it just one of those accidents, like so many that preceded it, brought about by Lady Fortuna when she chances to spin her wheel at random? Or was Siham ill, and unaware that she was crossing a busy thoroughfare on which the cars hurtled along too fast to stop easily should a driver be surprised by a woman in the middle of the road? Or did she dash into the path of a car, having decided to die on that particular day? Had she wanted her death to take place on Ashoura, or had she specifically wanted this moment to pass in silence, unnoticed by anyone amid the violence and turmoil, that her disappearance might itself vanish behind the collective fear of an impending invasion? Or had she chosen to anticipate the terror by her death because, though she had endured illness and pain, she could not face what was coming?

She was struck by a car — that much her family confirmed. How and why? I don't know.

In three days the news of her death would settle into some secret place — buried, invisible, or erased — where I would not see it or stumble across it. The air strikes on Baghdad, and the attack on Iraq by ground forces, began. Then came a telephone call at ten o'clock in the morning: 'Two streets away from your house there's a battle going on between students and security forces. The students are trying to reach the American Embassy, but the security forces have surrounded them and are beating them up. Some have been wounded – we're going to Tahrir.' A belated and hopeless effort to protest – so be it. Nadeem said he would go with me to the square. Hamdiya tried to dissuade him, then decided to accompany us.

We remained in Tahrir Square from one in the afternoon until eleven in the evening; the security forces left us alone to hold our demonstration there, interfering only when some protesters made renewed attempts to get to the two embassies – the British and the American – in Garden City. At that point fierce battles were waged with truncheons, tear gas, and fire-hoses on the part of security, and on the people's part the usual weaponry: such stones as were to hand. At eleven o'clock, the number of protesters dwindled, while that of the soldiers encircling the square increased. I went home with Hamdiya, but Nadeem went with his mates to a coffeehouse in Bab al-Louk, a few metres from Tahrir Square. I wanted to go home to listen to the news, because even while standing in the square or walking through it or chanting or talking to some of my old comrades, inside me the thought kept repeating itself ceaselessly that the event taking place there was far from a demonstration consisting of twenty or thirty thousand: merely a voice on the sideline, it would change nothing in the greater scheme of things.

I sat up until dawn, watching the scenes of battle being broadcast live on television via satellite. When I awoke at noon, Nadeem was not at home. Hamdiya said he had gone to Friday prayers at Al-Azhar Mosque; I guessed that he was going to join the demonstration that would follow the prayers.

Hamdiya said, 'Today is Mother's Day. Nadeem forgot to tell me "Happy Mother's Day". Nadir didn't ring, either.'

I was about to scold her for her foolishness, but I didn't. I said, 'Happy Mother's Day, Hamdiya – Happy Mother's Day three times: from me and from each of the boys until they give you their wishes in person!'

I made myself a cup of tea and then sat down by the telephone. I looked at my watch, with its hands creeping toward one-thirty. All at once I stood up as if I had an appointment, and got dressed. I told Hamdiya, 'I won't be late – an hour or two at most, and I'll be back. Nadeem will have come home and we'll have lunch together.'

I walked to Kasr al-Aini Street and headed from there to Tahrir Square. The square was peaceful, cars streaming through it as usual, although greater numbers of security vehicles had been stationed there of late. I turned right on Tahrir Street, making for Bab al-Louk Square, then went left toward Talat Harb Square. As soon as I got to Sabri Abu Alam Street I took note of the dense ring of soldiers blocking access to the square. I could hear, but not see, the large demonstration in Kasr al-Nil Street, apparently coming from the direction of Ataba, and Opera Square. Loud chanting. I tried to get closer, but the soldiers told me to back off. I moved aside, off the pavement, with a throng of pedestrians – they, too, were concerned about the demonstration and the invasion of Iraq.

The demonstrators proceeded toward Tahrir from the direction of Mahmoud Bassiouney Street or Kasr al-Nil Street. The security forces opened up the blockade and allowed us to move in the direction of the square. The two streets I had speculated the demonstrators were coming from – from one of them, that is – were still closed off. I reached the square, then turned left into Talat Harb Street. At the door of the Café Riche I saw one of my father's colleagues in a wheelchair and his wife standing next to him. I greeted them. The woman smiled at me, and the man wept. Perhaps he had been weeping before he saw me. Others were standing near him on the pavement. Then an officer came and ordered everyone to disperse. He said, 'Standing here is prohibited.' The woman pushed her husband's wheelchair, and I moved toward Tahrir. Before I reached the next intersection – the junction of Al-Bustan and Talat Harb Streets – I saw a row of security vehicles on the opposite side of the street from the Nasserist party headquarters, and I noticed the ground was wet, that there was in fact a great deal of water, along with a residue of stones – large ones, small ones, crumbled ones. Then I saw the dogs: big dogs, and with each dog a special guard holding it leashed by an iron chain. I carried on in the direction of the square and found the way to it blocked by a circle of helmets and truncheons. I retraced my steps to Al-Bustan Street. Traces of battle were in evidence there: stones on the ground, and water. My heart raced strangely, and I leaned against a car. I took a deep breath, then tried to breathe regularly. Suddenly I said to myself that something dreadful must have happened to Nadeem. I began to run.

How could I run, when moments before I had felt as if I was about to faint? How can I have paid no attention to the fact that any of the officers might have considered my running a sign that I was a demonstrator who should be arrested? And what route did I take home from Bab al-Louk Square? Falaki Street, or Mansour Street, or else I penetrated the neighbour-hood as far as Noubar Street and went by a circuitous route that took me to Kasr al-Aini Street and home from there.

'Where is Nadeem?'

Hamdiya said, 'He didn't mention anything about having lunch with his friends. He's late!'

By nine o'clock in the evening Nadeem had not appeared, so I began ringing up such friends of his as I knew. Some of them said, 'We haven't seen him in days.' Others said, 'We were together when the march set off from Al-Azhar Mosque. It was a big demonstration – security couldn't break it up until they set the police dogs on us and brought in special forces. We started running – we spread out into the alleyways and neighbourhoods, then came back and regrouped. When we moved from Al-Azhar Street to Ataba Square and from there to the city centre, we didn't see him – nor when we got to Tahrir Square. It was a big crowd, and we thought he must have gone in a different direction, away from the square.'

I rang up contacts of my own who I thought might have news about arrests or injuries. No news yet.

Hamdiya would not stop crying. 'Maybe they beat him at the demonstration,' she said, 'and he fell and got trampled. Or maybe,' she added, 'he was wounded and the police took him to the hospital. We must ask at the hospitals,' she said, and then, 'We should call Nadir to come and look for his brother.' She went on and on, and I shouted at her, telling her to be quiet so I could carry on with my telephone calls and inquiries.

She wouldn't calm down. I decided to go look for him. I went out with her, muttering to myself that she was an insufferable woman. We stopped in at the hospitals, starting with the Es'aaf Hospital and ending with Kasr al-Aini. At the first hospital Hamdiya lost no time asking about the wounded youths who had been beaten by the security forces during the demonstrations. I took her forcefully by the arm and whispered in her ear, 'They're not going to answer that question for you. We should ask whether a young man came to their emergency room hurt or wounded. We'll give them his name and description.'

We checked the emergency rooms from one hospital to another, in Al-Azhar, Ataba, and Ramses, and then we moved on to Kasr al-Aini.

When we got home I said to Hamdiya, 'Your idea wasn't a good one, Hamdiya.' She was still crying.

I went back to telephoning people I imagined might have information. After that there was nothing we could do but wait. I made two cups of tea and turned on the television to see whether there was any fresh news. Around noon the telephone rang. It was one of the friends I had rung up earlier. He said, 'Nadeem was one of the young men who were arrested. We sent several lawyers to the stations to find out where each person had been taken. We were told that they may appear before the investigator tomorrow afternoon. I'll get confirmation and let you know. We'll stay in touch.'

I conveyed all this to Hamdiya.

What happened then was the last thing I expected. It would never have crossed my mind that it could come to such a scene as what ensued upon that conversation. Hamdiya's face, already flushed from weeping, turned a still deeper red, and she began yelling at me, 'It's *your* fault! This is what comes of your talking to the boys about politics, all your droning in their ears. You've destroyed our household and lost us Nadeem. As soon as he comes home safe and sound and goes to Dubai I'm going to move in with my sister. Then we can go our separate ways.' She blew her nose, wept, and kept up her bizarre talk. I didn't know whether I should slap her across the face, shout at her the way she was shouting at me, or go out and leave her.

I ignored what she had said. I turned up the volume on the television and started watching the first press conference with Tommy Franks, the leader of the operations. He was saying, '. . . this will be a campaign unlike any other in history, a campaign characterised by shock, by surprise, by flexibility, by the employment of precise munitions on a scale never before seen, and by the application of overwhelming force . . . Our troops are performing as we would expect – magnificently.' A column of armoured vehicles crossing the desert. Huge balls of fire against a background of smoke and palm trees. American soldiers on the deck of an enormous battleship, cheering at the launch of the opening volley of tomahawk missiles. Tony Blair declaring that the Iraqis were an oppressed, humiliated people, and that Britain and her allies would bring them democracy and prosperity, and would protect their oil wells and refineries.

The following afternoon, we were unable to see Nadeem or any of his mates who had been brought in transport lorries to the national security courthouse, even though Hamdiya and I, along with other family members of the detainees, had gone early to the courthouse and spent two hours waiting on the pavement opposite the building. The blue lorries arrived, and queued so as to reverse in the direction of the door through which the boys would pass; thus they exited the vehicles and entered the building without anyone on the street seeing them.

It was then that I remembered, and knew that I had had a premonition of this moment when, months before, I had been following the transport lorries. My heart had told me. I would be following a lorry and staring through the opening and the heavy grillwork covering it, that I might catch sight of Nadeem's face, or he might see my face smiling at him.

The families were permitted to enter the building and wait in the lawyers' chamber. We saw the boys climbing to the upper floor to be interrogated, and then we saw them coming back down, toward the lorries. Then we were allowed to stand near the lorries, where we waved farewell to them, and they waved back at us, each one raising his two hands together to wave, for their wrists were shackled together by an iron cuff.

By the time Nadeem and his mates were released, Baghdad had fallen, and the Americans and the British had occupied Iraq. Two weeks later Nadeem left for the Emirates to work in Dubai and join his brother. He travelled on Tuesday afternoon. Hamdiya followed through on what she had said when she was shouting and crying like a madwoman, on that sad Mother's Day: she collected her things and moved in with her sister. On Thursday evening I got dressed and went to the New Generation Centre in Ain al-Sira to attend a belated ceremony that had been organised for Siham.

The hall was jammed with her friends and acquaintances, most of whom had taken part in the student movement, some from the College of Engineering or from other colleges, as well as cohorts from the period when she had studied in the Soviet Union, and others whom she had met at one time or another, leaving an impression upon them that drew them – despite the passing of the years and her protracted seclusion – to come and bid her a final adieu. Life in general – in our part of the world, at any rate – combines the funny with the sad, mixing the momentous with contrasting humour and whimsy, and so it was that a bunch of middle-aged people entered the hall, bearing the unmistakable signs of lives lived in trying and difficult circumstances. They were not shy about introducing themselves: they were the students who worked for the government, in the nineteen seventies, against the student protesters. Some of them had partaken in that memorable event at the College of Engineering, the day they surrounded Siham with clubs, insulted her, and told her, 'Get out, and don't open your mouth in this college'; whereupon she sat down on the floor and said, 'This is my college, and I'm not leaving. And I'll speak up here whenever I like. You want to beat me, then beat me.'

They revisited this tale, saying, 'May she rest in peace.' They said she was courageous, and had earned respect. It was clear from the expressions on their faces that they were genuinely affected by her death.

Chapter twenty-four

Siham

H ER PICTURE IS ON the front page of the book. Most likely it is a picture of her when she was still in high school, her first year there. She is wearing a dress that looks more like a school uniform, with buttons in the front and a round collar, one of those types known as a 'baby collar', maybe because of its association with children's clothing. Her hair is smooth, thick, and long, parted in the middle and falling to her shoulders, but not covering her forehead or her ears. Her complexion is white, her eyes light-coloured (the picture is black-and-white, and so doesn't reveal the green of her eyes). A long face with a broad brow, a small nose, and somewhat full lips; her face has grace and a sweetness, or innocence, or gaiety hiding behind an apparent seriousness and visible placidity. There is perhaps also a touch of sadness in this face, betrayed by a slight cast to the right eye that you wouldn't notice if you didn't look closely. In her ears are earrings, circular in shape – are they gold or silver? In a black-and-white photograph you can't tell for sure. A child, a girl, and a woman in the making converge in the picture.

Above the picture is her name, and next to it, 'Flower of the student movement.' A subtitle follows in the third line: 'The seventies generation.'

Beneath the picture are words in a fine, brittle script. (The confused scrawl of those who, like me, were educated at French schools, and didn't have handwriting teachers or get that strict training in the aesthetics of Arabic calligraphy.) The words read 'Love cannot be blind, for it is love that causes us to see' (a maxim she wrote in 1966, when she was in high school).

The book includes recollections offered by her brother and some of the leaders of the student movement, and women friends of hers who had shared life in a prison cell with her. It concludes with an appendix comprising fragments of her early writings, when she was fifteen years old, as well as some later texts, and Qur'anic verses she had transcribed with care. This included, under the heading, 'God', a list of twenty-two of His attributes as laid down in the Qur'an, beginning with 'the Merciful', and ending with 'Verily God is your Lord and greatest protector'. Following this, as a conclusion to the section: 'And God knows that which is within your very hearts.' Then there is a snippet in which she sees the world as a mountain that all people climb, each kicking those who are below, to prevent their ascending, and she concludes this thought with, 'Where is mercy, where is kindness?' Following this is a quotation from the words of Jesus: 'Blessed be the meek, for they shall inherit the earth.' In another snippet she writes, 'Give love instead of hate, and you are a point of light.' And, 'Smile upon him who strikes you, and give him a rose – thus you will be a soldier in the only true war, and you will be victorious because he was victorious. Jesus said, "Forgive them, Father, for they know not what they do." And where did he say it!'

There are two selections in the appendix written in 2002, exactly a year before her death, the first of them dated 14

March. In this one she acknowledges the twentieth anniversary of her decision to give up her graduate study in the Soviet Union, saying, 'The step I took so courageously was to reach for the sky, and nothing but the sky would have done,' and 'It's a decision I would take again if I could go back in time: a triumph of the spirit over the body, a triumph of light over darkness.' And, 'From that day on, despite all the hardships, I am still climbing the spiritual ladder . . . twenty years of genuine struggle, struggle in the name of God.' And, 'O Lord, guide my craft to the shore that lies distant.'

In the second selection, the date – Tuesday 26 March – is written in French, followed by an English expression, which she translated, 'The word "freedom" is merely an analogue, for man no longer has that which he has lost.' After this, in Arabic, 'The important thing is not for a person to be Marxist or Muslim or Buddhist or Christian – the important thing is to be an honourable Marxist, or an honourable Muslim, or a genuine Christian.' Then she talks about the stairway ever rising that we seek day and night, '. . . at demonstrations in the daytime, at night in reading, and in contemplative inquiry at all times.' She concludes, 'From one stairway to another, God has led me to climb toward His unmediated image.' On the next line, all by itself on the line, are the words, 'His radiant image.'

Her brother said, 'She was doing a lot of reading and writing. All through the years she wrote incessantly. She wouldn't leave the house. She read and wrote. All we have is scattered papers and notebooks whose pages generally aren't in any logical order. She left only a few notebooks. It's a strange thing, because she was writing all the time, and this went on for years. I don't know what became of those papers. Did she get rid of them by burning them? Was she tearing them up? Or was she tossing them from the balcony, the way she used to do with other things?

'Yes there was a period during which she used to throw her things from the balcony. She didn't want to own anything, anything at all – she would throw away clothing, keepsakes, and jewellery, among other things, and it caused problems between her and our mother.

'Sometimes she would overeat, or eat irregularly. She would gain weight noticeably. And sometimes she abstained from food, fasting for days at a time.'

'What about the zoo episode?'

'That wasn't the low point, although our parents saw signs of sheer madness. She was still able to make beautiful things, and wanted to – she wrote lines of poetry on the walls of her room. She did embroidery. She was good at embroidery, at making toys for children out of cardboard, and other things. One time she decided to take some coloured balloons and stand at the gate of the zoo to distribute them to the children. She talked about the policemen who demanded a bribe in exchange for letting her stand with the vendors who set up their portable stalls near the zoo. She was still capable of telling a story, of offering criticism and ironic commentary.'

Then came silence.

'She didn't want to talk. She was entirely silent for a whole year, barricading herself behind silence, refusing to talk to any of us.

'Before this silent period, she had been talking in a way that suggested she was approaching a state like that of a Sufi, or sometimes the things she said leaned toward Christianity, and sometimes just the opposite of all this.

'No, she didn't go into a convent, as some said.

'Yes, she attempted suicide more than once. She tried to jump from the balcony, but the neighbours saw her and she was rescued. In Paris, while she was staying with our mother, she swallowed a lot of pills, then went outside and fell down in the street, so she was taken to the hospital. Then she tried again, when she was in the hospital for a simple operation on her foot. She read in some magazine about spray guns. She sneaked out of the hospital, bought the gun, and tried to kill herself.

'We took care not to tell her about Arwa's suicide. We were afraid of the effect the news might have on her. Then she found out . . .

'For years we kept taking her to the hospital. She would undergo treatment. The therapy would leave her with a glow that quickly faded, and she would go back into hospital. She would improve and the doctor would say, "There's no need for her to stay." We would go home – in a matter of days or weeks, she'd go back. Yes, she gained weight noticeably. She refused to take medication. She would get rid of it; give up speaking altogether; go on hunger strike, and write.

'I don't think she committed suicide. She was hit by a passing car. In all likelihood she was completely oblivious to what was around her – perhaps oblivious to the fact that she was walking on a busy thoroughfare.'

Siham died on 13 March 2003. One week before the invasion of Iraq. Had she been following the news? Did she know anything about the approaching battleships, the massing of soldiers, the matériel? Did she decide to die so as not to witness what she saw was coming? Did she decide to die or was it a traffic accident? Did her brother say all that he knew?

The last of her extant writings that I have goes back to the year before she died. Dated 26 March 2002: she wrote about a feeling that was drawing her to write a book in which she would tell the story of her life – she described it as 'an important book, containing a warning,' but she stipulated that she wasn't looking to publish it. 'I don't like publishing, ever.' 'But,' Siham went on in her delicate, spidery script:

It's important to record the story of my struggle
Should I set down snippets of it, or chapters, in my
    memoirs
But it's a long tale, and multi-faceted, and besides
At any rate, I'll see how it goes
But I'll definitely get started
I won't publish everything
That's not for me

In another passage she writes:

Lord, all I ask is to become a martyr
So take my soul tomorrow morning
Before my eyes open upon another day
I've asked for martyrdom and even abstained from food
    and water for eight days.
And fewer than that and more than that.
A resistance whose cruelty only the honourable and pure
    know,
I've asked for martyrdom for the sake of truth
And now I can't find it.

Deliver me, O God
For suffering has been emplaced upon suffering
Upon suffering
I weep so often, this you know.

She was struck by a car on 13 March, corresponding to 10 Muharram. By accident or by design? I don't know.

Chapter twenty-five

The prison of life, the splendour of life

A T CAIRO STATION THE commotion, the disorder, the dirt, and the crowds take me by surprise. I stop by one of the stalls and look at the books on display. I reach out to an old edition of two of Tawfik al-Hakim's books, with faded covers: *The Prison of Life* and *The Splendour of Life*. I leaf through them, then put them back where I found them and buy some newspapers and magazines, which I place in the outer pocket of my small, wheeled travelling case. Pulling it behind me, I go past the platforms of the trains for Alexandria and the cities of the Delta and eastward, proceeding to the platforms for trains to Upper Egypt. I wait for the train. I see an attractive, sweet-faced woman striding resolutely, a little girl with a ponytail clinging to her hand. Walking beside them is a heavy woman carrying an infant swaddled in blankets. A middle-aged man with a heavy moustache and white hair smiles at the girl, who waits until her mother's attention is elsewhere to stick her tongue out at him. The train approaches. It stops. I board and look for my seat number – my seat is next to the window, and I settle into it. The train moves off slowly, then gathers speed and a monotonous rhythm. From the window I observe dilapidated buildings, heaps of rubbish, and the absence of any colours that are not faded or dusty or yellow. The train makes its way through a cloud of dust. Then we are past the villages of Giza and we enter the fields. Who was it that said to me once that the eye is also needy? The phrase consisted only of this ambiguous ellipse, and yet I understood. We were, as I recall, at the periphery of a city and approaching Dahshour, where we were met by palm groves, the colour of the palm fronds that uncertain shade between pure green and a subtle, mysterious silvery hue. The yellow of the laden branches of the fruit-bearing trees was liberally interspersed with a lovely red. Yes, the eye is needy. From my window now I see, not palms, but the expanse of long fields, divided into rectangles and squares, each containing such crops as its farmer cultivated. I laugh suddenly, and a server from the buffet stops by me, thinking my laughter is meant to summon him. I wasn't thinking of ordering a cup of tea. I order a cup of tea. He pours the boiling water over the tea bag and stirs it with a spoon to dissolve the sugar, then presents the cup to me. I am smiling again, watching the little girl with her mother in the train. Between one sip and another from my cup, my thoughts turn to Nadir and Nadeem. Nadir laughed, and Nadeem cried. Nadeem had wet himself. He said, 'I want to go to the toi –' but he didn't complete the sentence. He wet his seat and the moisture began to flow in a thin trickle down the leg of his trousers. Before Hamdiya could open her mouth to scold him, I grabbed her hand and gave it a squeeze. She understood. I admonished Nadeem good-humouredly and said to his brother, 'This happens to everyone. Let's go wash up and put on some new trousers.'

I carried him in my arms to the train lavatory. The residual odour of the child's urine clung to my dress throughout the journey. I had washed my hands and my neck, but I couldn't very well repeat history – take off my dress and exit the lavatory in my underwear. When my aunt greeted me with an embrace, I began to laugh out loud. I whispered to her, 'Aunt, you'll have to change your clothes and take a bath before you go to afternoon prayers. The front of my dress is soaked with Nadeem's urine!' I laugh again, and for the second time the buffet server pauses by me. I'll have to tell him that, when I want to get someone's attention, I call him, just like everyone else on God's green earth. I shake my head and tell him, 'No, thank you – I don't want anything.' I extract the newspapers from the pocket of my case. I swallow my daily dose of poison; I must admit I have a strong stomach – I can take it.

I move rapidly from one newspaper to another, then open a magazine in which I read a quarter of an article here and a few lines of one there. I fold up the newspapers and magazines and put them under the seat. It's not littering – they'll collect them with the rubbish when they tidy the train – surely they must tidy the train from time to time! I close my eyes.

The boys went to work in Dubai. Cairo or Dubai – what's the difference? Besides, that is, the salary and the relative ease of day-to-day life? But the apparatus is what it is. Was it Foucault who said this, or is it a quotation he cited in his book, the one where he characterised prison as the deployment of a system's power over a person's behaviour, his freedom, and his time, every day, day in and day out, year after year. It decides for him when to wake up and when to sleep,

228

when to work, when to eat, when to rest, when to talk and when to keep quiet. It defines the nature of his work and the required level of productivity. It dictates the movements of his body, and appropriates his physical and spiritual resources. Such is prison, albeit with variations. Here or there – it makes no difference. I close my eyes. I keep them closed, thinking maybe I'll have a nap. Perhaps I do nap. I look at my watch: between the time I closed my eyes and when I opened them five minutes have elapsed. I have a long way to go. I observe two women sitting on the opposite side, to my left across the aisle. One of them is wearing a dark-coloured dress, which drapes a flat chest and a long torso. She is lean and stiff, with a hard face and her hair pulled tightly back and secured behind. The other is full-figured and looks amiable, her body generously curved, and she wears a multi-coloured dress. She has left her hair free to wreathe her face in ringlets. Are they sisters? I smile at this foolish notion, and then pursue it: maybe they're twins. I steal furtive glances at them and establish the difficulty of determining either woman's age – it is as if they were ageless. Something about the way they sit makes them seem rather like statues – it's odd: two ordinary statues on adjoining seats in an express train. The skinny one looks straight ahead as if staring into space, or as if she were sightless, blind. As for the plump one, her gaze takes in everything. For a moment, they appear to be two strangers who just happen to be riding the train together, and then all at once they bend at the same moment, inclining their torsos just slightly and whispering for a good while, as though colluding in some affair. I look at the stern one and a shiver of fear pervades my body. I shift my gaze to the other, and relax at the sight of her kind face, her matronly curves.

I gaze out of the window at a prospect of fields, which blurs things, and the women's two images merge. I murmur the Qur'anic verse, ' "No fear, nor shall they grieve." It's just a couple of women I happen to have seen in the train.' 'The two of them,' I think, 'are going to dog me for the whole journey.' I chide my heart for its forebodings: what ill omen can it find in the two women? I look away from the two of them and go back to Nadir and Nadeem. I miss them. The idea that they live so far away confounds me. Especially Nadeem. Will he never have the chance to become what he wishes? Hamdiya is a fool and a dolt, but she's kind — she'll come round, calm down, and the waters will resume their course; perhaps the boys will come home, get married, and then will come the grandchildren. I laugh, and steal a glance at the aisle. Thank God, the buffet-server isn't in this car at the moment.

A curious anecdote could amuse Hazem for an entire day. I was going to tell him about the two women, tell him they seemed like an apprehension of destiny split in two. He would make fun of me, just as he did the day I told him about the crow. He said, 'I'm a student at Al-Saïdiyya School, but I skipped school to take part in the sit-in,' and he didn't laugh. Like an idiot I believed him, and all the while he was a pre-med student, looking after his mother and three brothers — he was five years older than I was. Shazli held it against him that he wanted to be a successful doctor — and what would Shazli have had him be? An incompetent surgeon at whose hands people would be transformed into the crippled or the dead? My heart skips a beat when I hear anyone mention Hazem, saying, 'An exceptional surgeon,' or 'He taught me . . .' or 'He helped me . . .'

or . . . I will hear nothing but good spoken of him, and sincere prayers for his soul.

And Shazli? An odd coincidence. An unexpected encounter in Prague. He said he was working in tourism. 'What are you doing in the tourist business?' He was pleased with himself, driving a fancy car, smartly dressed. Perhaps he wanted to dazzle me with his newfound wealth, or perhaps he imagined that I would regret not having accompanied him in his triumphal march. I had escaped – my God, but I had escaped! Why is it that we credit Lady Fortuna only with the catastrophes? Why not give her her due, when at a stroke she saves us from breaking our necks?

But there's no place for Fortuna here: it was something of reason, common sense, intuition, the intelligence of the heart. I took to my heels and ran. Arwa could have run – why didn't she? Her legs betrayed her. She was ill, so how could she run? Perhaps she was influenced by the words of that French thinker who saw, in suicide, the attainment of a great person's victory, an event rather like a grand play without an audience.

And Siham? She withdrew to her room, a small room, two-and-a-half metres square, a solitary confinement in which she spent twenty years. Meditating. In torment. Reconsidering. Looking for a way out, at one time thinking, 'I will assemble that book in which, without a doubt, there will be a path for the godly'; at another time beseeching, 'Forgive them, Father, for they know not what they do.' Back and forth, back and forth, until the search exhausted her and she surrendered to fatigue and quietly passed away. I often find upon my lips the words, 'Forgive us, Siham.' I said to my mother as I stood upon her grave, 'Forgive me.' I had left her to die alone, far away. I close my eyes and I see her at the great demonstration on the thirteenth of May 1968, walking amidst men and women with their hands joined, advancing in a row as wide as the street, with lines of marchers extending all the way from the Place de la République to the Latin Quarter. I still don't understand why my father said she was an anarchist, or why they separated, she a beautiful woman and he a fine man. I see a three-year-old girl insisting that they swing her, her mother taking her by the feet and her father grasping her under the arm so that she stretches like a bridge between them, and they swing her. The girl laughs, laughs loudly and long, and when they stop and put her back down on the ground she says, 'Again!'

A girl coming home from school goes in and joins her parents – a big girl now, in middle school, she shows them her composition book and the final grade she has received for it. The important part is the teacher's comment: 'I have never given a final grade for expression – this is the first time, and Nada has achieved it.' One ought to be delighted, to laugh, but modesty calls for something else. The girl settles for a smile.

I look at the two women sitting across the aisle, who are exchanging whispered conversation – I wonder what they are saying? I go back to stealing glances at them and notice that each of them has, at the same moment, drawn from her bag a ball of wool yarn. The severe woman's is dark grey, while the genial woman's is blue, somewhere between sky-blue and sea-blue. Next appear two pairs of knitting needles, to each of which is attached a swatch of worked wool already done and settled in the women's laps. Rapidly and mechanically they begin moving their hands and arms, each pair of knitting needles likewise active as they work.

I look at my watch. I look out of the window. I draw from my bag a book in French I had begun to read two days earlier, in which the author recorded his experience at Tazmamart Prison, in the southern desert of Morocco. There were fifty-eight men from the officer corps and the rank and file of the Moroccan military who had been imprisoned on a charge of attempted coup d'état against the king. Upon their release, after the eighteen years of solitary confinement imposed on each man, only twenty-eight of them had emerged from the prison. Thirty detainees at Tazmamart died. They died from torture, hunger, illness, and madness. Some of them died of disabling diseases in their solitary cells where there was no one to help them eat or go to the toilet or wash. I had stood in the classroom where Ahmad Marzouki, author of the book and former inmate at Tazmamart, told of Lieutenant Shamsi, who, after years of incarceration, took to beating his head against the bars, calling the names of his daughter and his mother, and he kept calling them until he died. I open the book to the page where I left off. I can't find it in myself to read. I think, 'I'm going to see my aunt.' I close the book and put it back in my bag.

I see my aunt spreading her arms wide and enfolding me. I kiss her head. I say, 'I'll be staying with you for two weeks, Aunt.' I look at my watch. I steal a glance at the two women, now completely absorbed in their knitting, not exchanging a word, not looking at the wool in their hands, just continuing to work on it. The severe woman's face is rigid and harsh, like a face without eyes or ears, while the plump woman's face is cheerful, overflowing with tenderness, as if she were listening attentively to someone telling her a moving story.

I look again at my watch. 'Almost there,' I murmur.

Epilogue

Farag

T HE OCCUPANT OF CELL number ten at Tazmamart Prison tells us of a memorable day that the inmates of cellblock number two witnessed – it turned their lives upside-down.

A few months before that day, a flock of wild doves had alighted on the prison, on the roof of which a dovecote had been constructed. The inmates greeted this news with mixed reactions. Some were fearful of ill omen, certain that wild doves lived only on grave-sites, among ruins, and in desolate places – they referred to popularly held belief to the effect that doves bring death in their wake. Others were fearful that the doves' chicks would attract snakes. Still others were hopeful, and reminded their cohorts of Noah's dove, the olive branch, and the good tidings it brought.

Then on the second of August the inmates heard the sound of something falling from the roof. Those who were still able to move about and walk approached the doors of their cells and looked out through the slit. They saw a spot of white on the floor of the corridor, which they surmised was a bit of cement dropped by the guard, or it might be a snake – was there such a thing as a white snake? When the guard opened the cell doors to distribute the daily ration of water, Marzouki reached out quickly and seized the white object before the guard could catch him at it.

The guard locked the cell and left.

Marzouki cried, 'It's a dove chick!'

The news flew to each man in his cell – from cell to cell, and then came the details: It was nearly naked apart from its downy fluff. Its feathers were new and tiny, and only on its back. It was trembling. Its leg was bent and its head drooped on its breast. Its heart was beating, beating intensely. There was a swelling on its side. It had fallen a long way – it was about four metres from the prison roof to the floor.

Marzouki called out, 'I'm naming him "Farag!" '

Marzouki poured a little water for it into a plastic dish and watched it drink. Then he crumbled a bit of bread for it, which its tiny beak couldn't pick up.

As Marzouki tells it, 'From that day forward, everything I set out to do was altered. There was no longer anything that so preoccupied me as the dove chick's well being. In this regard the most delicate and fragile of all concerns was its nourishment. I would take a piece of bread, moisten it with a few drops of water, break it into bits and knead them into something resembling grains of wheat, then leave them to dry for several hours. So that the chick might eat, I would grasp its back carefully, open its beak with my right thumb and index finger, and introduce two or three pellets of that artificial grain. It would readily swallow the stuff, beating its wings and cheeping, asking for more. Its shrill chirping could be heard by inmates of the most distant cells, who all called out, "Bon appétit, Farag!" '

Marzouki took to subtracting from his own scant meals whatever was necessary: peas, lentils, fava beans, and tea

– which Farag especially loved and accepted with alacrity. Inmates of the other cells sent along whatever they could. It was good food; Marzouki contented himself with intensely savouring its aroma, but did not permit himself to eat any of it. Farag came to have three meals a day, then four, then five.

Marzouki writes, 'Days passed in this way, and Farag grew marvellously: his beak got stronger, and in place of down grew beautiful grey feathers; a white patch took shape distinctly on his back and his leg healed completely. Then one day he turned toward his food and ate on his own. After that he was able to climb up onto the cement bench. I felt like a father – I took to spending my time contemplating him in wonder. On another day, in one go, he flapped his wings and alighted on my shoulder. I let the other inmates know, and they whooped with joy – even those who were semi-paralysed – and called out to him, each from the other side of his cell wall, congratulating him.'

They all began discussing Farag's future. Should they release him in the corridor dividing the cells? What if the guards caught him and killed him?

The majority decided that this was a risk worth taking.

The inmates assembled, each taking a position behind the opening in his cell door, and they observed as Marzouki attempted to release Farag from the narrow slit in his own door. When he had successfully accomplished his mission, they saw that Farag was frightened for some moments, beating his wings tremulously in alarm, before he took off in flight; the men cheered and applauded him, raising up their mingled shouts of encouragement. It seemed then that their fervour touched Farag himself, for he took flight in the corridor, swooping back and forth, all eyes upon him – they had even stuck their hands out through the openings in the cell doors, and eventually Farag landed upon one of those hands outstretched toward him. The inmates cried out in exultation. Farag looked at Marzouki, then flew toward him, alighting on his hand. Marzouki drew him inside carefully, an hour before the guards were to make their rounds. After the guards left, the inmates called for Farag.

'What are you waiting for? Let him out!'

Once again their hands reached out. Shouts of enthusiasm and delight were intermingled with exhortations, 'Come here, Farag – here, over here, come to me!'

Because Farag was important to all of them, the inmates decided that he would have his own special account, and so each of them paid into it what he could; through the agency of a co-operative guard they were able to purchase grain necessary to feed him. When he became ill, for him they dissolved in water those tablets that came so dear in prison: lozenges of aspirin and vitamin-C.

On a Tuesday, Marzouki recalls, with the help of a friend of his, he undertook, by means of a complicated procedure, to release Farag altogether from the prison building.

When he announced the news the other inmates were furious. 'You had no right to do that,' said one of them. 'You should have told us first. I won't ever forgive you for what you've done – you've broken my heart!'

The day passed in silence, and the night likewise.

Then in the morning someone cried out, 'Farag's not gone! It seems he spent his night under the roof of Building One, and that he's looking for your cell!'

The bird enjoyed a hero's reception.

Farag began coming and going. The prisoners kept tabs on what they took to be his battles with other doves. They saw his feathers scattering and falling before their eyes. 'Persevere!' they shouted, 'Keep at it!' 'He's dead,' they declared, then, 'No, he's fine,' they said. He came back to them exhausted, feathers plucked out, after his first attempts at life on his own. The third time Farag went out he was gone for a week; then he returned and tried to get back inside. The inmates addressed themselves to him: 'Take heart, Farag. Get your head in through the bars, then your body, and there's an end of it.' On the final occasion, with the help of a broom handle, an inmate succeeded in getting Farag outside the building's bars. Again he came back, and this time he wasn't alone. Accompanying him was a mate, an elegant she-dove, as Marzouki saw her. He wrote, 'She was slender, with a small head and gleaming feathers – a beautiful female.' This time Farag didn't try to get in. He was puffed up with pride and self-confidence. His mate took fright from the shouting, and flew off. Farag stayed behind a little while, then caught up with her.

Marzouki says at the end of this chapter of his book, *Tazmamart, Cell 10*:

Farag built himself a nest beneath the roof, opposite cell number ten, and produced three broods of chicks.

On the day of our departure, the fifteenth of September 1995, though it was difficult for me to move, and despite my tremendous excitement as they removed me from the cell I had entered eighteen years earlier, I paused to look toward the roof. 'Farewell,' I murmured, 'and thank you.'

A NOTE ON THE AUTHOR

Radwa Ashour is an Egyptian writer and scholar born in 1946. She is the author of numerous novels, short story collections and academic works and contributed to the essay collection *Reflections on Islamic Art*. A long-time professor of English literature at Ain Shams University in Cairo, she holds a PhD in African-American literature from the University of Massachusetts at Amherst. She lives in Cairo and is married to Palestinian writer Mourid Barghouti.

A NOTE ON THE TRANSLATOR

Barbara Romaine has previously translated three novels, including two by Radwa Ashour, as well as Bahaa Taher's *Aunt Safiyya and the Monastery*. She has also published shorter pieces by Ibrahim Aslan and Mohamed Qandil, and translated some selections from classical Arabic poetry, which are forthcoming in literary journals. In 2011 her translation of Ashour's novel Spectres was runner-up in the competition for the Saif Ghobash Banipal Prize for Arabic Literary Translation.

A NOTE ON THE TYPE

The text of this book is set in Bembo. This type was first used in 1495 by the Venetian printer Aldus Manutius for Cardinal Bembo's *De Aetna*, and was cut for Manutius by Francesco Griffo. It was one of the types used by Claude Garamond (1480–1561) as a model for his Romain de L'Université, and so it was the forerunner of what became standard European type for the following two centuries. Its modern form follows the original types and was designed for Monotype in 1929.